ITHACA: THE NOVEL

ITHACA: THE NOVEL

Z. K. Goat

atmosphere press

for Mary Ann Malinchak Rishel,
fiction writer, humor scholar,
colleague, and friend
for more than 40 years

Keep Ithaka always in your mind.
Arriving there is what you're destined for.
But don't hurry the journey at all.
Better if it lasts for years.

– C. P. Cavafy, "Ithaka"

There are heroes in the seaweed....

–Leonard Cohen, "Suzanne"

A sudden blow: the great wings beating still....
A shudder in the loins engenders there
The broken wall, the burning roof and tower....

—William Butler Yeats, "Leda and the Swan"

People either loved that country and couldn't imagine
living anywhere else, or hated it, left it as soon as they
could, and never came back.

–Robin McKinley, *Spindle's End*

"Those are swans, princess," said Tenedos.

In such a shape had Zeus visited the mother of Helen. How white Helen's skin must be. How long and slender her throat. How graceful her profile.

We walked on. I dreamed of swans and cold clear gods.

"Swans are vicious," said Tenedos. "Be careful of swans, my princess."

—Caroline B. Cooney, *Goddess of Yesterday*

The embalmed white moth in the lavatory of Room 214 of the Argos Inn continues to fascinate Penelope. In its little black-framed box it seems to stare down at her, tiny specks of eyes preserved through time, the eight dark orange spots on its wings even more like eyes, as though it were a miniature of the monster that gave name to this place she and Odysseus have been living in all summer. Today the moth even seems to glare at her. She shivers. She has never understood why her husband gave his beloved dog that dreadful name before he sailed for Troy. Tribute to another hero and *his* ship? *Men*....

Moving easily back into the white room with its long draped panes of glass, she selects her favorite garment–an ankle-length short-sleeved gray cotton dress imprinted with a large owl–which she acquired one Saturday morning in early June from Silk Oak at the Farmers Market. As she pulls it on over her head she watches the room's current living occupants turn a bit in their sleep. Odysseus is still snoring between them–silently, of course–and she knows they have no idea why they are dreaming of wind-tossed green waves.

In her usual way, she glides through the locked door with its cunning brass nob reminiscent of a sea urchin. The time is 6:40 a.m. and she knows the lovely young man with music buds in his ears has begun to set out the scones and croissants and fruit in the dining area below this room. Again she offers a quick prayer of thanks that the arrangement with Hades, while requiring invisibility with Athena's help, allows her and her husband corporeal pleasures when they so choose. She certainly does enjoy the fat sweet blackberries the inn has been providing, and every day she takes delight in eating as many as she desires before breakfast time officially begins at 7 a.m.

Alone on one of the polished benches she sees through the wide windows that the sky is moving between gray and blue, storm and clear. *The fifteenth of August*, she thinks. *Our time here is almost done.*

⁂

With a final snort, Odysseus awakens and sits up. A slant of light is gleaming through the room's heavy curtains, but the couple in bed with him is still sound asleep. One of the men is holding the cream-colored fake-fur cover bunched up like a toy bear. The other has both arms bent above his head on a pillow. Odysseus easily extricates himself from them and goes to the john.

He doesn't really need to pee, of course–though he could if he wanted to–but he likes looking out the window at the sign across the street: ITHACA COFFEE COMPANY, with a big red cock set to crow. He likes being reminded of where he and his wife are, that this city was named after his home—well, indirectly, thanks to him.

The Argos Inn feels especially quiet this morning. *August 15*, he remembers. Has it really been eleven weeks since he and Penelope arrived? She's already left for the day, of course, to walk the few blocks uphill to her writing room at the top of Seneca Street. He marvels at how she can stay so focused, sitting all those hours. Well, she did it at her loom, too, he knows, year after year while he was gone, good Hellenic wife that she is. Not him. He's got to be *moving*. Even all that time with Calypso....

With another yawn and a stretch, he looks down at his body. Muscles still firm enough. Hair gone silver, but still thick. Thigh scar still prominent–and dong a living wonder–but then he chuckles. *Dead a long time*, he reminds himself. Telegonus and the stingray. But hey, here he is, far across the world, all because of his wit and cunning. He snaps his fingers. *Attaboy, Odd-I-see. You've done it again.*

He slides into some loose Flax pants from Trader K's and an old blue cotton shirt and grabs his Ithaca Beer Company cap. All for his own enjoyment, of course. *You won't want to be seen in Ithaca* Athena told them, and she's been using her power to keep Penelope and him unobserved as they enjoy their stay in the Finger Lakes.

He chuckles again as he exits the room to descend the dark brown stairs and grab a cup of coffee from the breakfast area before leaving the inn. He's glad he can enjoy food and drink if he chooses to. *And no one sees dead people,* he thinks. *Ghosts are invisible.*

Four and a half miles northeast of the Argos Inn—less,

as the falcon flies—the Novelist has awakened and risen at her usual early hour to make herself a good breakfast. Through her kitchen window, she notices that the sky, after a heavy rain, is set to offer blue instead of Ithaca's too-usual gray. Her invisible little owl, companion since her time on Skyros, has perched himself next to her canister of Gimme! Coffee; both are just over eight inches tall. Sleepily he rotates his head one way and then the other. He relishes the smell of a fresh brew, she knows, and it helps him to stay awake at least a few daylight hours.

The Novelist places two scoops in her French press. Next to it waits a gold-rimmed white mug printed with a piece of a poem about the town she's lived in for so many decades. She reaches for a small waxed box of cream, a tin of cinnamon. Through her window she sees the male cardinal return to the hanging feeder again, crimson above white blossoming roses, a black sunflower seed in his beak.

The Novelist has shaped a satisfying life. Some envy her, and some may resent her successes, but most revere her, and she knows so many interesting people and so many famous people that she can ignore whom she doesn't please and whoever doesn't please her. (And it isn't true that Gore Vidal once made her cry at the Key West Literary Seminar. She was sneezing.) Even after a good span of decades she continues to be fascinated by the lives of people around her in the world.

Today, however, she feels again the anxiety that has poked and prodded her all summer since her return from her simple but elegant winter home on the island at the southernmost edge of the United States. She is poised and eager for a breakthrough: what will her new book be? Another collection of stories? (The one about ghosts went out of print until a sensible publisher picked it up again.) More essays about children's literature? (She was *central* to getting the world outside of England to celebrate Angela Carter. How about a focus on Australian Angela Slatter now?) Another collection of her favorite book reviews? (She's given away most of her copies of the first.) Popular nonfiction, like her books about clothes and houses? She shakes her head. None suit. And certainly no poetry, she thinks with a shudder; she's certain her first and last attempts, while she was an undergraduate at Radcliff, had all the non-quality of watered-down Auden. No, she wants the engaging experience of writing another novel–but something *different*, even *odd*. She certainly has had stretches of time this summer with her longtime Beloved in India again collecting folktales. And even her commitment to start teaching a graduate course at Cornell again in a couple of weeks, while significant, will leave her plenty of time for her own writing. *Plenty of time.* She thinks of her imminent birthday in early September and winces a bit. She's stopped counting.

Looking out of the window again, as the aroma of steeping coffee fills the room and elicits a warm "gwooooohk" from her little owl, she is suddenly struck with a dismaying recollection: Virginia Woolf's character in *To the Lighthouse* (based, the Novelist eruditely knows, on her father) who is in constant agitation because he cannot "get to the letter Q" in the alphabet, meaning he cannot advance in his intellectual endeavors. The Novelist sighs. May-be *she* is stuck that way, too? Her last novel, about an elderly swimmer in Key West, did not achieve strong critical success, though she's aware many readers-of-a-certain-age rightly applauded it. Has its relative lack of acclaim held her at *N? Can* she at least move to *O* and *P?* Surely she can get that far!

After a pat on the head of the little owl only she can see, she shrugs her shoulders and takes a small saucepan from a cabinet. *I want an egg* she has realized. *Soft-boiled. With pepper and salt. And butter. And two slices of toast with raspberry jam.* After all, she's entitled.

�◆〰〰〰

Ghosts are invisible, Penelope reminds herself with pleasure as she makes her way east on Martin Luther King, Jr./State Street for the climb northward on Schuyler to Seneca. *Good for my thighs*, she reminds herself again with a wry smile as she turns east again to continue her ascent.

She is so very happy she found just the right place for her writing retreat. Not only Ithaca, with its literary centuries, its university and college, its community that celebrates the arts–but this single room high at the top of Seneca Street in a buttercream-colored house full of student rentals, a room she does not even have to share with a live human being because no one sublet it for the summer. She delights in the outer walls with their curved shingles shaped like the scales of a mermaid's tail. She delights in the fire escape landing where in May she immediately set out three pots of sweet low basil. She delights in the lustrous green leaves of the tall maple trees that reach as high as the peaked roof of the old house and define the view from her small window over the worn wooden desk where she sits to work at least eight hours every day. She delights most in this reprieve from the Underworld with its cold shadows and hollow echoes and too-often-repeated stories. Her poetry has been thriving here.

Those trees are still dripping a bit from the night's rain, she notices as she approaches the house to drift through the door and climb the creaking stairs. *I'm glad*, she thinks with satisfaction. *It's good for the basil.*

After a few limbering stretches she sits at her desk. All her notebooks and pens–also invisible to others, of course, thanks to Athena, in case the landlord should make a visit– await her neatly. She has had excellent success with her efforts this summer. She brought with her drafts of old poems and has written a good number of new ones. Now that it is almost time for her and Odysseus to return to the Underworld, she must review them, test the woof and warp of the overall manuscript. *Can* it be considered a longpoem? *Should* it instead take shape as a chapbook of individual poems? *Might possibly* it eventually become a full-length book, an intricate tapestry of words, especially if she and Odysseus were again to trick their way into a retreat away from Hades? She shakes her head over that last possibility, though. *Not likely, no, not likely at all. That god is a selfish son-of-a-bitch. She's talked enough with Persephone to know for sure.*

Regretting Pomegranates

Again Demeter folds her summer robe
imagining Hades flexing his muscles,
maybe putting on a black leather vest
to show off the tattoos her daughter hates:
dead owl, crossed swords, bloody poppies.
A new one writhes on his right bicep:

huge scorpion curled to sting. God
of shadows, he dictates dim light, but
each year when his stolen bride returns
he allows her fat candles, flames,
so she can see how his lust has grown
all the time Earth's trees have bloomed:

Demeter knows he'll grab her daughter
greedily at the last dank step, sink
his teeth in, mewl and maul, then
slam the door to the living world,
laughing again at the harvest goddess
swelling tight white core to ripest red.

Pretty much every morning Odysseus has taken this
stroll westward through town to the inlet past the highway.
Nothing like a good swim to start a day. Not his beloved
Ionian Sea, of course, but a hell of an improvement over the
River Styx.

Where he likes to swim is illegal, but no one ever
bothers him, of course, thanks to Athena. Amazing how she
still watches over him and Penelope after all these
centuries. He's always been a lucky cuss.

He thinks now of how hard she laughed when he told
her how he'd stymied Hades with a riddle and won these
summer months away from the Underworld.

"What *was* the damned riddle?" she had asked, already
smiling.

Odysseus had enjoyed taking his time to share it. "I

asked him, 'Have you ever found a clock in the sand?'" He had no idea what I was talking about, of course. It isn't even a riddle. But he was so annoyed at himself and also intrigued that he just had to know the answer, and that's how I finagled a vacation for Penelope and me. Of course, I also had to promise to bring him back a unique gift."

Athena, he recalls, had stared at him with wary eyes as she asked, "And what *is* the answer?"

"Ha! A trick one, of course: 'No, but I have lost many!'" Odysseus had told her triumphantly. He hadn't made it up. A crazy-mustached Spanish painter fellow had shared it with him about thirty years ago soon after dying. They were sharing red wine. Lots of red wine.

"Just watch out, Odysseus," Athena had said with a shake of her head. "Sometimes you are just *too* clever. Even heroes make mistakes."

Odysseus had nodded then, but now he smugly grins. The inlet's waiting for him. Onward!

H ◆ ≋ ☺ ♍ ☺

After breakfast and a shower, the Novelist puts on an embroidered blouse and a long full skirt, all gentle greens and blues. Her hair is pure white now and in her mild vanity she likes to emphasize it. When she reaches for her favorite shoes– simple black flats, like ballet slippers but with a sole, very comfortable–she notices one is definitely finally splitting. *Well,* she muses, *Fontana's must be having its annual sidewalk sale by now. I'll stop by Eddy Street later today.*

She goes downstairs and looks through the window again. Not far from her large lawn statue of a sheep, three deer are fearlessly grazing on the flowering bushes in her big backyard. They have the run of the place, especially because the bordering land belongs to Cornell for plant experimentation. No hunters allowed. With disappointment, she sees that no viburnum blossoms are left: deer appetites have expanded along with the size of their population.

Q, she thinks again. It's haunting her. And what of *O* and *P*? Yes, she should go into her study immediately and turn on her computer (ignoring all email messages) and *write*. But she just can't make herself do it. She's full of an unusual restlessness. She needs to get out.

GreenStar's already open, she realizes. She's just used the last of the whole wheat bread and also finished the jam, too. Good reason not to try to write: she wants to be sure to get a fresh loaf of her favorite Wide Awake Bakery bread before it sells out.

The sky's gone gray again, so she decides on a light raincoat. Carefully she places the little owl–still fairly awake–inside the deep left pocket of the coat. She exits the house she is so fond of and gets into her car.

A travel book? she wonders. But she's looked through her old published essays and articles about places she has visited; they feel dated, boring. *Maybe a novel based on my times teaching on Skyros?* Institute co-founders Dina and Yannis would like that, she's sure–as long as it didn't have the snarky satire D.M. Thomas used for *Lady with a Laptop*. She might enjoy drawing from how, on another fifteenth of August, before an earthquake closed off the path, she and her Beloved had climbed to the small temple to Athena overlooking the Aegean. In pagan times it had been cut, cave-like, into the lava-plug mountainside. The day she visited it, in its ruin, very small crumbling chunks of its white marble still lay about, clearly just abandoned rubble, and the Novelist had picked one up and put it into her bag to bring home in reverence. She's kept it in a special place on her desk ever since in Athena's honor.

Would her sharing this story offend people? No, who would care? The temple had long ago been converted into a Byzantine chapel, with beautiful gilt paintings of saints on the walls, and then *that* worship had been abandoned. When she was there, she saw that scaffolds had been pushed right into the deteriorating portraits. Folks at the Skyros Centre told her, when she asked, that there *had* been money from the government to restore the paintings, but it had dried up, so the workers had just rammed their equipment into the cave and left.

The Novelist hasn't thought about that day in years. Why is Greece in her mind at all? Why today?

Suddenly restless, Penelope pauses and gazes out her window. The sky she can see through branches is still pale gray and blue. She stands up and runs a finger over the dusty sill, then pulls up the sash. The fresh air suddenly sets her mind on a poem idea she's been struggling with, something Odysseus told her about his boyhood. She decides to try a title and write in prose what she can recall:

Odysseus Remembers His First Experience with Death

He was five years old, playing with stones, throwing them, strengthening first one arm and then the other. He used small ones first, white and round. Gathered from the sea's edge, they were smooth and bright and felt good in his palms. Then he looked for larger ones, and larger, working to throw them just as far as he had thrown the small ones. What he doesn't remember was whether or not he decided to hit the goat. Small and black, it wandered towards him from behind some olive trees. It made no sound as the stone took it down, so surely did the sharp gray weight connect to its forehead. Odysseus stood there, not knowing if he felt powerful or surprised, nor which of his hands, his right or his left, had thrown with such sure force.

As she writes the words, she seems to be living the moments herself, or at least dreaming them as if she were her husband. She grins. "Comes of a good long marriage," she says aloud. Then suddenly–as though it has needed that paragraph to be able to launch itself into her imagination–she fills more than a page with an entirely different new poem. But why this island she has visited only in dream and story, so far from the Ionian Sea?

Skiros

How did the goat die?

It stepped too high, too fast.
Thunder threatened from the sea.
It bleated once, twice
as air rushed past its belly,
slope crumbling in its fall.
Lightning struck.

Where did the goat die?

An edge of Skiros named Atsitsa.
Gray stones, red rocks, green waves
still calling out for young Achilles,
his mother's salty tongue.
Flat weeds dried out by long sun.
A rough stretch, full of thunder.

Why did the goat die?

She was chosen.
Or she wasn't.
No one can say for sure
if gods demanded hoof and horn
or if death simply came to her
in that fast summer storm.

When did the goat die?

As rain began to hit him.
As a rooster began to scream.
As last light left his open eye
and journeyed out into the clouds
that gathered over his pale curves
still warm where his blood stilled.

What goat died?

No one's. Everyone's.

The island holds them on dry hills
that cry for rain and thunder.

He was old. She was young.
It wore a jangling metal bell
someone found at Palimari.

Who saw the goat die?

Everyone. No one.
Thunder moved through olive trees
and rain dropped high and fast.
She was prayer. He was supper.
It gave its unknown name forever
to all who journey here to climb.

As he makes his way through the center of Ithaca, its shops and most restaurants still closed, Odysseus grimaces again at the ugliness of unreasonably tall buildings being built. As it is, people already have to endure hideous black iron structures–like huge dead cockroaches–at each end of The Commons, as well as signs that shout out "NO" as their first word. Large planters of gorgeously arranged flowers cannot compensate for the disturbing lack of beauty caused by construction. He can only wonder what the heart of this small city looked like years ago when a miller decided to found a university here, or even when a conservatory of music started to become a college.

He and Penelope could have gone anywhere. It was she who became charmed by the idea of spending their time in the city named after their island. Even so, they could have chosen another Ithaca in another state of America. But she had heard that this one in New York, at the southern end of one of the Finger Lakes, was a place where many writers have come to study and teach and where many have chosen to stay because of that lake and the gorges and the hills, and the open community and the politics, and the Farmers Market and–oh, her list had seemed endless. So here they were. Her for inspiration. Him–well, for a goddamned *break* from the lack of sun and wind and clear water that he's endured for so many years. He's needed the freedom to put his body into *motion* again.

So here he is, away from the gloom of the Underworld, enjoying another gray-blue-gray probably-humid-later day in a town known for enlightenment. It's still early enough that few others are out and about. Odysseus frowns again at the monstrosities of steel girders and gets past them as quickly as he can. Painful memories of certain giants from his past...and dear comrades lost. He decides to jog awhile, but gives up, wheezing after a block or so, and walks the last five to the inlet, past the Rhine House, over the railroad tracks, past GreenStar.

Next to Finger Lakes Electric, at 804 West Seneca–he continues to be fascinated by these numbered buildings–a concrete bridge spans the water. Today a blue heron is perched on it, seeming to stare at him (which he knows is not possible). Could it be Athena come to greet him? What might she have to say today? But when he approaches, the bird startles and takes flight. An actual bird, then, not the goddess. What has it seen to make it fly away?

Odysseus is used to slowly swimming laps between this bridge and a companion one a bit north that is part of

Buffalo Street. He's enjoyed trespassing—"Smile! You're on Camera!" an illustrated sign announces—by climbing down the five metal steps on the side of the building that lead to the water. Now he strips off his clothes and starts toward the pipe railing.

But suddenly a man in coveralls rushes out of the front door of Fingers Lakes Electric and with a sharp voice cuts into his calm. "Hey, buddy! Whaddya think yer doin'? You ain't allowed to swim there!"

Odysseus stops still in shock. *What the hell? What happened to invisible?*

ᚻ◆ᵐᗡᴔᗡ

The GreenStar parking lot, this early, still has available spaces. Across Route 13 and the railroad tracks a wall of bright colors catches the Novelist's eye. *When did somebody paint a mural there?* she wonders. She thinks it looks a bit like the beautiful Cornell poet Alice Fulton.

As she steps out onto the pavement she wishes she hadn't risked wearing the worn-out flats, because the left one splits a little more as she starts to walk. *Fontana's for sure*, she muses.

Before entering the store she stops outside to examine a special exhibit of organic herbs in pots, drastically on sale because planting time is far past. *Maybe some basil or rosemary for the kitchen?* she thinks. *I could keep it right outside the door.*

As she's considering, a striking-looking man passes her on his way into the store. He's not handsome, exactly, and shorter than most, but he walks with such assurance that she can't help but take notice. And, damn it, isn't he *Greek?*

His dark eyes and body shape take her right back to her times on Skyros. He glances at her with an odd expression on his face, and in her pocket she feels her little owl stir.

Yes, some basil and rosemary would be good, she decides and picks up a pot of each to add to her intended purchase of bread and jam. Before she goes inside she looks up at the sky. *Those clouds are certainly thick and heavy now,* she observes. *That happened fast.*

⁂

After reading the new poem aloud, Penelope sets it aside. But it's got her thinking of her own island. Hills of goats, groves of olive trees, shores ragged with rocks and pebbles polished by centuries of sea. From a folder she takes a sonnet she's been drafting for a while.

Stones

The pink ones draw us first, that rose of dawn
from sleepless nights of love remembered, full
and perfect as smooth Aphrodite's shell
and just as sea-swept as two hearts alone.
The green ones next, deep dark cat's eye at noon
or ancient pines left standing safe and tall
with roots stretched deep into a rainless hill
above the remnants of an ocean shrine.
Our bodies bend with fingers reaching out
to touch the curves of color, wrest them free
from wave-tossed sand into our hands where hot
and dry transform their brilliance to pale gray.
More softly now they offer inner gleam,

a weighted wisdom, talisman of dream.

How different from Ithaki is this *Ithaca*, a city next to a deep lake carved out by ice, in the middle of New York State in the United States of America, many hours from any ocean. Again she shakes her head, smiling. Ithaca. Ithaca. Echo of her marriage island, her near-widowhood island, her palace of woof and warp and a growing son, where in rare moments of leisure she liked to rest on the seat her husband had carved for her in a stony mound close behind the palace. When Odysseus–always-clever Odysseus–tricked Hades into giving them a reprieve from the Underworld, how was it they were able to come *here*? She thinks she's figured it out. Forays to the county library and to Buffalo Street Books and to Autumn Leaves have shown her that poets and novelists and essayists who have lived or still live here have journeyed to the islands of Hellas to write and to teach and to give readings. It's become her cherished belief that their visits have shaped a kind of portal that she and Odysseus—with Athena's help, of course— were able to use to travel here. Not that she has any proof of her certainty–but she's confident she has always had good intuition.

How naked and surprised, Odysseus finds himself speechless as he stands by the inlet. Incomprehensibly all he can think of is *clock in the sand, clock in the sand,* and Hades saying, "Okay, you two, okay. I'll let you out of here for a while. But I'll know where you are."

He stares at the man who spoke to him–who can *see*

him. The stranger seems to be both scowling and smirking, with a wry gleam in his eye, standing there as though mocking him. Then, through the blotchy whiskers and mottled skin and balding head, Odysseus suddenly recognizes...Hermes!

The god dissolves his disguise and laughs. "Gotcha, sailor! But you'd better take my word as a warning. You've been just fine until now, doing what you want, you sinner, but today people will watch you do it."

Odysseus regards his great-grandfather with distrust. *Always a trickster....* He can't get a grip on the god being here at all. Athena, yes–but why the slippery guide between the worlds? Then a grim thought hits him: is Hades calling him and Penelope back to the Underworld earlier than promised?

"Athena's not here, kiddo. Didn't you see the sign she left you?" Hermes pokes his thumb back towards the wall of the Rhine House. Squinting, Odysseus can see something painted on it, but not what. "I think maybe she thought that portrait would take her place, but it ain't so. Nope, there's trouble in your paradise today, my hearty. Your protector's off celebrating at an anniversary party. Today marks Mary's Assumption into Heaven. You must know the Mother of God's pretty much her direct descendant."

Odysseus certainly has *not* known–why the hell would *he* pay attention to Christianity?–and he continues to be confused. For the first time away from the Underworld he feels exposed, vulnerable, out of control. He reaches for his clothes. Hating even to think it, he has to ask: "Can't you take her place today, Lightningfoot?"

Hermes is already shaking his head. "Not my job, buddy. Not my responsibility, no sirree. I'm just the messenger. Besides, I kind of like the idea of Athena maybe getting into trouble with Hades over it." He pauses. "You should thank me. At least I let you know. And maybe I'll check in with you later. I'm gonna stay around a bit. I'm kinda liking this town. I hear there's a *fab* hair salon called Transformations...."

Odysseus has to content himself with those words because Hermes, like a spark snuffed out, has completely disappeared.

⚜

Noise on the roof of the organic grocery store lets the Novelist know that rain is now falling heavily as she continues to wander the aisles. She has realized that, yes, she really could use a few more groceries, maybe to make a special meal for herself as encouragement to decide about her new book. A farm-raised chicken to roast with butter and lemon? Some ground pasture-raised beef and a couple of eggplants–she knows she has onions at home, and cinnamon and nutmeg, but is she up to making a good bechamel sauce? Turning and backtracking among the now-crowded aisles in what feels like growing confusion, she locates fat garlic, a dozen tiny potatoes, a new bottle of virgin olive oil, a block of feta, a jar of whole Kalamatas, bulk walnuts, some oranges for zest and local honey for a cake....

When she moves to the meat section to look for lamb and begins to wonder if GreenStar has any goat meat available, she literally stops still, almost knocking over a woman wearing a tie-dyed head scarf and Birkenstocks. *Goat meat?* Again the little owl–how possibly still awake?–

rustles a bit in her pocket.

Feeling decidedly odd now, she finally finds her loaf of bread (one of only two remaining) and selects not only her favorite raspberry jam but a jar of imported grape jelly, too, and finds herself speculating on the likelihood that she could persuade GreenStar to start carrying Mythos or Fix if a beer importer could get it.... *Well, there's always Discount Beverage for a case of retsina....*

Almost in a small panic she hurries to a register. She's brought only one cloth shopping bag, not anticipating her extra purchases, so she has to take a paper bag as well and do her best to carry with one hand the now rather bedraggled basil and rosemary.

How long *has* she been listening to the rain fall? She's lost all sense of time. Now she feels the wind gusts, too, as she stands in the store's foyer, its doors open. She doesn't have an umbrella, but she decides she just has to get away from the store, so–despite it further damaging her shoe–she rushes to her car and practically tumbles into the driver's seat, her bags and pots barely intact as she struggles to protect the little owl in her coat pocket, now hooting softly in alarm.

August 15, she suddenly remembers. *The Assumption of Mary.* Her Beloved had mentioned it that day of their climb, said how fitting it was to visit that day. *Athena's temple.* So that's why she suddenly wants *dolmades*?

♓ ♦ ♒ ♋ ♍ ♋

Intuition has gone far in helping Penelope shape her manuscript. For now she is calling the body of her new work *Of Swans*–a broad enough title, she figures, suggesting the history she is working with. How long ago did Zeus lust for her aunt? Could he have known (imagined, planned, feared, hoped for) all that that single feathered coupling would engender? Gone he was, in an upward sweeping blur, the moment after. Wings into thundercloud, beak into lightning to strike elsewhere at his whim. Through the centuries Penelope has had time to find and consider just about every other writer's interpretation of this satisfaction of lust that led to the Trojan War. And this summer she has penned her own, exploring truths and half-truths, memories and dreams, giving herself free rein to set the story down her way. She thumbs through her manuscript to reread her efforts.

Leda's Legacy

There was, it is said, a girl named Leda,
a young woman chaste of heart
with eyes like lakes of glass.
Zeus, arrogant god of air, desired her
and in his practiced cunning took
the shape of a beautiful bird, a swan
of great proportion and grace,
and flew down to the earth.
For Leda loved the water lilies
and daily wound them in her hair,
lingering long on the moss-soft bank
to watch the swans in their gliding dance
upon the silver water.
                  Some say
that when the giant bird approached

she tried to run, to beat him away.
Others claim she embraced his wings
and coupled willingly. None know
the truth: rape or spontaneous love.
But to the daughters conceived that day
she gave each a flower saved from her hair,
and a strange smile touched her mouth.
Those who saw swear it is so:
one blossom glistened like rounded gold;
one gleamed like cloth of purple.

Penelope has imagined a hundred times or more what the world was for her aunt until Zeus chose her. Freedom. Choice. Strength of her body in youth. No fear that she would be singled out, descended upon, forever changed.

Leda, Before

She is swimming through the morning
lake and no one else is there. Black weeds,
green weeds slide across her skin but she
is not frightened, moving and moving through
the silent water. No one else is there. Her hair
sleeks back from her face. Her arms reach strong
and sure. On the shore behind her wait the dress,
the woven sandals she removed. They are dry
and safe on the safe, dry shore. No one else
is there. No god, no swan to make the swim
a poem. She knows nothing but clear water,
clear air, taste of morning, wide sky
deepening from rose, blossoms firm
on her journey's edge. She dives
once, dives again, surfaces
clutching a single round
stone she knows she will
keep forever, forever
swim through the
summer lake, no
story but the
touch of water:
breath,
muscles,
cool,
blue.

Still nonplussed, Odysseus stands still for a while, looking at his surroundings with new eyes. People can see him! He can no longer go wherever he wants, take whatever he fancies, enjoy others' foibles without their reactions to him. No more invisibility. But if his great-grandfather is telling the truth–always a gamble, that–it's for only this one day. A new and very disturbing thought strikes him: *Penelope, too!* Surely she's safe in her writing room and went there so early that probably no one saw her? But what about when she goes out for lunch...?

Resolutely Odysseus reaches into his pocket and pulls out the coins stolen a while ago from a loud-mouthed magician's busking basket on The Commons. He has not needed them, of course, but has been amused by carrying them around in his pockets as souvenirs, maybe to take back to Hades. They make a nice jingle. Today he'll have to *buy* what he needs. and now he needs to purchase food for Penelope and get it to her before she decides she wants to eat and leaves her room.

GreenStar has been a haven for them with its excellent fresh organic food when they have chosen to enjoy eating. Odysseus–glad they open at 7 a.m.–makes his way through their parking lot and towards their fragrant foyer, remembering to smile blandly at anyone who notices him. A woman in a raincoat, standing at a wooden rack of late-in-the season herbs, stares at him as though very startled.

The coins won't buy much, but he's able to afford a couple of vegetarian egg rolls wrapped up with little cups of sweet and sour sauce that will fit in his pocket as he walks the length of Seneca Street. For amusement he's counted his steps on earlier walks: 1,152 from where he is now.

When he crosses the railroad tracks he understands what Hermes was talking about. The western wall of the Rhine House used to be blank. Now a large portrait of a woman with long black hair and wildcat eyes stares at him. Rainbow mountains surround her, with a pale purple one at the top: Olympus, surely. Full lips seem to try to be whispering something to him, a warning, an apology. Hermes may find this embarrassed attempt entertaining, but Odysseus can only groan. If Athena thought this portrait would console him, she was way off this time. She must have been in a rush.

Sighing resolutely, he keeps heading east. But what's this now? Damn! One of his Scirian sandals has started to separate where a toe has pushed hard against the weave. He's walked in them at least a thousand miles over all these years and they've withstood rough rocks and the salt spray that soaked them as he stood poised at sturdy prows. And *today* they have to start falling apart?

The heavy summer storm of the night before has darkened the sidewalk and bent branches of full green trees downward from their sunward reach, and now another one is threatening, filling the sky with dense gray. He has to step more carefully where the concrete squares riddled with many winters' cracks offer a slippery deception of wet leaves and tumbled twigs. Maybe he should just walk barefoot? But there are too many dangers on the ground.

⚐

As rain pummels her windshield, the Novelist feels

released from a kind of dream. *It began when I saw that man,* she realizes. And again, with a tickling in the back of her neck, she thinks again about the alphabet. *O, P...Q.*

Suddenly she knows she must return home right away to write. Other errands can come later. The heavy sky, the Greekness–surely–of that short man have stirred her mind.

Curving up towards Cornell from Stewart Avenue, she recalls the long-ago day her old friend Allen Ginsberg came to town to give a reading. *Autumn of 1982?* They'd been comrades in New York City, so she'd felt no compunction about inviting herself into the interview he was holding with a local reporter and a doctoral student writing about the performance of poetry for her dissertation. She remembers he was delighted to see her again, and that they spent the time they needed to catch up while the other two humbly waited. She also–perhaps too vividly–remembers that as she drove to the site of the interview she passed *half* a squirrel trying to drag itself across the road after, apparently, having just been run over. Yes, it's the place on the road she's just driving over now.

Shuddering a bit–the darkness of memory sometimes! and after decades–she continues the few miles to her house. On Hanshaw, as usual, she encounters only a couple of other motorists. The little owl is sound asleep, so she does not turn on the radio. What news this day? She'll read her copy of *The New York Times* later.

At home again, with the rain abated, she parks her car and carries in her unexpected groceries and little herb pots. The latter she sets out on the small patio behind her kitchen, checking to see if they need watering. They do not. *They'll like the moist air today,* she thinks–then recalls the long dry summer days of Skyros where such plants thrive. *Oh, well.*

Tidily she stores her other purchases in the refrigerator and on a counter for later.

After carefully extracting the little owl from her pocket and placing him–still asleep–in a corner of the kitchen counter, she glances at the clock: just after 9 a.m. A good time to write–with a sweet cup of tea this time.

In a few minutes she's upstairs in her study, the tickle still at the back of her neck. *O, P....*

After straightening her desk, moving a box of tissues, pulling out a bag of stale jelly babies, adjusting a stapler, refilling a flowered tape dispenser, and spilling out a small tray of paper clips inexplicably littered with mouse droppings (*how? when? totally repulsive, especially to a Virgo*), she is able at last to turn on her computer.

Which she suddenly turns off again.

Somehow she feels compelled to write with pen and paper. More oddness! She roots out a lined notebook and a ballpoint advertising T-shirt Express. Yet no words come. None! She doodles, making circles, spirals, patterns like cobblestones....Stymied, she stares out through her screened window at the full-leaved maple she had learned was planted by her home's first owner just as the construction of the house was completed. Why, as she squints her eyes now, does it seem to resemble a weathered olive tree?

⸎ ✦ ⋒ ♋ ♍ ♋

Penelope has not been reluctant to enter with her poetry into the thoughts and feelings of the deity who impregnated her aunt, the great god who satisfied himself and thus set into motion the war that left so many wives alone–for years or forever–as it destroyed so many human lives. She has strived to develop negative capability, freeing herself of narrow ego, working to understand others' perspectives in order to achieve the beauty of truth.

Zeus

How best to best her? Mornings now
I watch her walk from house to shore,
hips swaying in the green of her

soft dress as though to beckon. Take
the shape of sunlight in her hair?
A butterfly, wings bright, feet sticky

on her palm with dawn's first nectar?
Too frail. I want to feel her feel
my coming. Wings, yes, to allow

descent through air, her startled eyes
upon my sudden flight. White dove?
Pure lust in love's disguise. Black

crow? A curving feathered dive
to fleeing golden hair at edge
of lake. I like the color–

but size, size! I need
a bird of weight, aplomb,
to hold her to me, ease
this burning ache.

This summer in Ithaca she has dared, too, to enter into her aunt's experience, to take herself to the mindset the woman might have had when she realized her inescapable fate as creatrix of a daughter whose beauty would so darkly alter the world. With her sonnet, she has answered the Irish poet's famous question that would make a mere passive vessel of her aunt's womb.

Leda Comes to Understand the Rain

After the feathered rush, the thrust of wings
that changed time for all time, I moved alone
beyond the place where love is god's brief moan
and every cell in woman's body sings.
A pregnant virgin's learned a thousand things
no man can comprehend, though on the stone
of marriage he has writ her name in bone
and blood, and bound her hands with precious rings.
Who am I that I dare to use my words
to mock? Call me true mother of all war,
call me the Muse, the one who's touched the birds
and come back down to earth as sacred whore.
My power is the knowledge that I hold
the future in my fragile egg of gold.

And surely in pregnancy Leda's nights must have changed as her swelling belly affected her sense of self, her imaginings, her strengthening into resilience, preparing for birth....

Leda's Dream

Where lake meets dusk, a woman with strong hands
calls fire from the shore where geese descend
in heavy clamor. On her forearms, bands
of burnished silver mirror far day's end
in rippled water. Seven willows lean
long leaves in aching arcs torn wild with wind
a young girl's never felt where spring's pale green
is all she's known of feathered and of finned.
The woman's eyes scan wave and depth for reach
of light gone lavender past burning peach,
where mallard mother undulates to teach
small ducklings unseen dangers of dark beach.
Sun's gone; a single gull cries last reprise.
The woman's fingers glow in gold moonrise.

One July evening, relaxing with Odysseus in front of their rented lake house, maybe after sipping a little too much ouzo as they admired circling fireflies, she'd gotten the crazy idea–who knows why?–to pretend her aunt had another sibling besides good-natured Althaea. Before she could sober up and dismiss the notion, she had had to go inside right away and give voice to that fictional being.

Leda's Sister and the Geese

All the boys always wanted her, so
it was no surprise about the swan-
man, god, whatever he was. That day

I was stuck at home, as usual, while
she got to moon around the lake
supposedly picking lilies for dye. Think *I*

would have let some pair of wings catch me,
bury me under the weight of the sky?
She came home whimpering, whined out

the whole story, said she was "sore afraid"
she'd got pregnant. Hunh. "Sore"
I'll bet, the size she described, and

pregnant figures: no guess who'll get
to help her with the kid or, Hera forbid,
more than one (twins run in our damned

family). "Never you mind, dear," Mother said.
"Your sister will take on your chores."
Sure. As though I wasn't already doing

twice as many of my own. So now
I clean, I spin, I weave, I bake,
fling crusts to feed these birds I wish

to Hades every day; while she sits smug
in a wicker chair, and eats sweetmeats,
and combs and combs that ratty golden hair.

She can't help but feel a little strange about that one.
Usually she's so serious! How much further afield might she
dare to imagine? *After all,* she reprimands herself, *aren't*

your poems trying to share the inner truths of what the world has come to call mythology?

Shifting the egg rolls a bit, resisting the temptation to bite into one, Odysseus pauses for a moment to study a huge spray of weedy roses that have burst through a low crumbling wall. He thinks of snapping off a few for Penelope, but then realizes they are the fragile kind that will disintegrate into loose wilted petals at even a careful touch. *Besides*, he thinks dolefully. *Now someone might see me steal them.*

That's when the storm hits. Not just a few drops, not like a small shake from the sky. Zeus-style: a downpour, a torrent, as if out of nowhere, with a huge gust of wind. Grimly Odysseus recalls the words he's heard from the famous Tompkins County band, The Horseflies: "I live where it's gray...."

Cursing now, Odysseus hops with some difficulty over a rapidly forming puddle. Now that he's corporeal he's getting drenched. He sees a few people dashing through a doorway and decides to join them. One nods and smiles at him as she shakes off an umbrella onto a worn mat inside. He awkwardly nods back.

It's clear to him that this building has felt the feet of many, many people. There's an energy he can't quite figure out: helplessness and yet hope. He gets a memory vision of emptied wineskins. What is the shock of this sudden visibility doing to his mind?

People are moving into a large high-ceilinged almost cave-like room, some with tentative smiles, others offering warm greetings, some straight-faced, almost ashen-looking. They are taking seats in a circle of folding chairs–maybe two dozen, Odysseus estimates. What should he do? He can hear it's still pouring outside. He takes a seat, careful not to crush the egg rolls. Maybe no one will ask him who he is.

A leader starts talking in welcome. Odysseus hears a phrase with which he's very familiar from all of his sojourns after the war in Troy: "One day at a time." Also the good advice–which he has often followed with Athena–"let go, let God."

People start to take turns speaking. Some are calm. Some cry. No one gives their full name. They talk of loved ones in trouble with alcohol and with other drugs, too. Odysseus has read about heroin–the fruit of the poppy–killing many, especially young men and women. He thinks of Telemachus, kept safe, even later with Circe....

Suddenly the person next to him stops talking. It is his turn to speak. What name should he give? Surely he should not use his real one. Grasping, he recalls a sign on Seneca Street he has passed by, outside a business that offers printing services.

"I'm Gnomon," he utters calmly. "I had friends–fellow sailors, I called them–who were lost to the ways of the lotus. They were my mates, and I felt they had betrayed me in their addiction. I struggled with my anger at them. They wouldn't listen, couldn't listen, just wanted that sweet escape.... "

It's a tall tale he goes on to spin–truly a giant one–but with one eye slightly closed he can see the others in the circle nodding sadly in recognition as he entrances them with his embellished memories. And with what he's going through right now, he can again live easily with the guilt of lying. People around him are nodding. Some are crying. Carefully he brings his epic tale to a close.

Two cups of tea later, one Earl Grey, one Tazo mint– with a couple of walnut sugar cookies she happily found in a canister– the Novelist is still sitting in her wingback chair with a spiral notebook opened across a cushioned lap-desk. Several failed starts at paragraphs have resulted in a carefully printed alphabet both across and down a lined page. Just as she begins to feel the urge to color them with crayons, she literally shakes her head and almost shudders in a dramatic gesture of self-admonition.

"Oh, fuck it," she says aloud and sets the lap-desk aside with a sigh.

Kicking aside her worn-out shoes, she moves to her bedroom for a sturdy pair of sandals and then goes downstairs. The owl opens one eye and closes it again. The Novelist wonders if it could be a good time to telephone her Beloved in India, but she can't remember exactly when, in India's time, he's scheduled to give his guest lecture.

A swim, she thinks. *That's exactly what I need.*

Wishing she could just magically transport herself to the excellent public pool in Key West, she knows that for laps here in Ithaca she usually has to make do with what Cornell offers inside. *Does* she really want to bother? Or drive all the way to the other side of the lake, where by noon the park will be packed with families? And after that storm this morning, what about the weather? She longingly recalls her hours on the huge white beach below the village on Skyros....

Again: "Fuck it." The owl wakes up. The Novelist reaches for the phone. She can always leave a message.

Penelope stands up and walks three times around her room, a pattern she has developed to help clear her mind. All well and good to write about her forebears, but what of her own story? She's never forgotten that Tennyson fellow, soon after his death, reading aloud his seventy lines supposedly in the voice of her husband (using that other name she has always rejected). With a small smile, she takes out the autobiographical poem she wrote when she first settled in at the top of Seneca Street and rereads it. *These* stanzas are her signature, she believes. A bit vainly she likes to imagine rhapsodes performing her words for audiences. *Who* is *my audience?* she suddenly asks herself.

Penelope

The world remembers me for loving him:
sleeping chaste in Ithaki, my heart firm
as the living tree he carved for our bed.
Good Penelope! Faithful and cunning wife
to fool with woof and warp
the suitors who would claim
all that Odysseus left behind.

But a woman doesn't love a man
gone twenty years, patience be damned!
I learned to love myself and lived

alone, as some might call it, manless,
supposed to weep and dream of his return.
Return? I knew that someday he might find
his way back home, that I'd be here;

yet in the interim there was no loving him,
for love is deeds, not thoughts and feelings
fluttering through the brain and blood.
What I wove on my loom I wove for me.
I dedicated every story in my threads
to bold Arachne, to all women brave enough
to spin the truth of history. At night

I smiled to hear the green and golden song
of growing skeins as I unraveled
images for the next day's telling.
Alone? When imagination looked toward dawn
as toward a secret tryst? When hands
grew daily stronger and more sure
that what they wove was powerful?

My stories broke the silence of the air
around the house, around the women
who watched them with a serious delight
and turned to one another, their eyes bright
with recognition, daring *yes*.
The suitors grew uneasy, called for wine,
insisted that the women dance for them,
and gradually as with one mind
began to shun the room where I sat weaving.
They sensed the presence there

of some new spirit–a calmness
in my smile, a way I had of gazing
at their leering faces unperturbed–
that disconcerted them, sent them away

muttering that something was amiss.
They couldn't read my loom,
saw nothing there but colors
meeting in confusion, if they looked at all.
So it went on. Years passed. I grew
older with the women, and together
we taught their daughters how to weave.

A hundred eager hands reached for the threads
and they surpassed my art so far
that I sat back in gladness knowing
silence would never still the air again.
It was that gladness, not time,
that drove the suitors wild
to claim me, shouting "Choose! Choose!"

And I would have chosen–to save us–
despite my son–had not Odysseus returned.
When he slipped into the hall in rags
and strung the bow, already I
loved him again, willed his success, welcomed
night embraces in the great carved bed.
So, loving, we continue.
And mornings, loving,
every loom a tree of light,
I weave again with the daughters around me,

fingers sure in time's glad reach,
learning from them now, faithful
to the green and golden stories
that celebrate our love.

Yes, she can't help but smile with satisfaction over that one. But suddenly a memory intrudes, a harsh experience she has tried to suppress, about the day Odysseus' goddess appeared to her as she was weaving.... With a deep breath, she picks up her pen. *Another sonnet—the right tight form.*

Morning, with the Suitors Close Below

As woof and warp give weight to weaving loom
and colors deepen under guiding hands
a clear light fills the open-windowed room
where suddenly severe Athena stands.
Penelope is silent, waiting for
a word of hope or fear about the man
who long ago should have returned, the door
still draped with black since when the war began.
This goddess here, his friend—a boon, a curse—
at last will tell her why his ships are late?
Long calm, harsh sea, wild winds—or even worse,
an unnamed terror as her husband's fate?
"It's time," Athena says, "lest you would lose
Ithaki for your son. Yes, now you choose."

Suddenly aching all over from the memory, she has to push the new work aside and lie down on the room's uncovered bed. But she can't rest. Needing to switch focus, she gets up again and randomly pulls from its folder an earlier poem. What surprise might arise?

Penelope Wonders, Waiting

What Beast will I find
if I open the door?
The turquoise door where

peonies blossom, ants run wild
in spring rain. Ithaka
is a safe strong island—

but that was long ago.
Now the ghost of my
love, Odysseus, makes his

journey again without me
while I write up the hill.
A long poem. A

good poem? Brightly
woven of all I am
and all my ghost can be. But

what of that dangerous
irresistible door
as twilight bends day's dreams?

Who's waiting there, demanding
my beauty? Marriage
is not what it seems.

Now where did *that* last question come from?

"Inner truths of mythology, my ass," she mutters, wishing she had a bottle of Aphrodite white to uncork.

She shudders a little and is tempted to tear up that poem and the other two just written–but no. She has to trust the place at the back of her head where words take shape in mystery. Let the editor in her forehead wait.

⁂

After the meeting, Odysseus sheepishly nods goodbye to a few people, still sharing their commiseration with him, and slips out the door. The sky has cleared and now warm humid air surrounds him. As he continues walking he feels a hankering for a smoothie from Shortstop Deli, but then remembers he spent all his coins.

Sighing, he tries to adjust his sandal. A fat squirrel stares at him from a branch. Usually he enjoys the squirrels–Ithaki offered only rats–but today this one with its twitching tail feels like an omen. His time in Ithaca is almost over. Crickets, coneflowers, mums, flowering sedum: all scream that summer is passing.

He encounters no one else walking for the next few blocks of Seneca Street, but car traffic heading toward Route 13 is a bit heavier than usual. Students already moving back? Buying used bookcases and couches from Mimi's Attic? Cayuga Street divides Ithaca's west from east, and there Odysseus stares dolefully at the abandoned Masonic Temple and, beyond it, again the horrific half-finished high structures that will accommodate new residents who have much more money than the downtown workers who would *like* to be able to afford to live in their city. Better to regard instead the Dewitt Mall, former school saved by a far-thinking compassionate individual whose vision made possible the creation and survival of Moosewood Restaurant, Dewitt Café, The Bookery, Buffalo Street Books, Guitar Works, Pastimes, Toko Imports, Made in Ithaca, and other small businesses locally owned. Odysseus appreciates care and concern for one's own; his hard work on his land before the war was what made possible Penelope's survival of the cursed suitors' invasion. He smiles now at the sign for Cayuga Coins, a shop where one day he found what is now called "an ancient," a disc of metal so old that Odysseus easily recognized it.

A block more and he pauses to gaze up at the *completed* large hotel sporting banners of Cornell University and a coffee shop depicting the face and breasts of a mermaid. Odysseus chuckles. He doubts very much that the sign designers have any idea that the first mermaid was the sister of Alexander the Great, who jumped into the sea to try to kill herself in shame for hurting her brother but who could not die because she had accidentally drunk the water of life for which he had so arduously journeyed. Or, for that matter, that the sirens were the lost handmaids of Persephone, living to revenge themselves upon all men because their cherished friend had been abducted by Hades. All the coffee company cared about was that people complained about the "obscene" split tail of the mermaid, so the symbol changed to just her torso and head. More giants, the business kind, who'd as soon throw down rocks on the world than lose stockholders and cash.

Pausing across from the Bernie Milton Pavilion, where he and Penelope have enjoyed Thursday evening concerts,

Odysseus picks up a copy of the *Ithaca Times* at the TCAT bus shelter. He's still not used to people looking at him and has to keep reminding himself not to stare at others. It's okay to gaze at the mural of five early Iroquois enjoying corn and strawberries. And he can linger a little further on at the corner of Aurora Street where Collegetown Bagels is full of happy customers. If only that damned sandal weren't slowing him down.

As Seneca Street begins to slope upward, Odysseus considers making a detour to the Argos Inn to try to fix his sandal, but quickly realizes the front desk clerk would not allow him just to walk in and head up the stairs into Room 214. Instead, he tries to change his pace to a fuller stride. He feels his thighs rub together a bit. *Muscle?* he wonders. *Or a bit of fat....* His skin has remained deeply brown from all his years of sun, despite the Underworld, and he is always reassured by the look in Penelope's eyes that he is still smoothly attractive to her. And to other women? Ithacan women? Hmm...today he might find out.

He passes a few pots of red petunias and then a purple door to a basement apartment with the phrase "Purplefish Properties, LLC" above it. Sadly it makes him think briefly of his second son and the stingray tail, but then he laughs when he looks across the street and reads another sign: "True Insurance." As if there's any guarantee against fate.

There's enough light in the sky for him to know it's midmorning–a bit early, he realizes, for the tantalizing aroma that's filling the air. When is the last time he smelled pork cooking over embers? He's been walking by some prettily painted homes, but now before him, on the southern side of Seneca at the corner of Schuyler Place, is a plain white one. Three wide concrete steps go up to a flagstone path that leads to the front door. On the westward side of the house is a small unpaved driveway. A window that looks to be eight feet high is partially obscured from view by messily trimmed bushes. Intrigued, Odysseus thinks he discerns much movement of small creatures behind the glass.

But it is what–who–stands in that otherwise empty driveway that captivates his attention. Beneath a canopy to guard against rain, a breathtaking beauty is grilling thick chops. A long apron printed with–wolves? lions?–protects the thin summer dress that enhances her perfect curves. Odysseus cannot help but cross the street and stand at the edge of the unmown yard. As if at a signal, the woman turns to meet his gaze.

Her eyes are every color of the seas he has encountered, shifting hues, an underwater kaleidoscope. Her smile shows no teeth, as if she is reluctant to reveal them. Her hair seems to lift off her neck as though it is blowing in an island breeze. Odysseus rapidly blinks, fearful his mind is tricking him. When he looks at her again, she is a normal twenty-something, probably a Cornell Hotel School student refining a recipe.

"Hungry?" she enquires.

And at once he is enormously so, almost beyond choice, the fragrance of garlic and black pepper and rosemary infusing him with the largest appetite he has experienced since the years he was alive.

"Yes," he says. "I am." Then he pauses, thinking perhaps she is a street-food vendor. "But I have no money."

She laughs. "No problem. I can see that you are Greek, too. We know what hospitality means. Sit down."

Then he notices she has placed two chairs by what he

now can see is a door leading to a well-lit ground-floor apartment. Again he observes much movement through the tall window. *Cats*, he realizes. *Many of them. Maybe she's a vet student?*

He sits and she offers him a blue plate with three chops on it, then hands him a fork, a knife, and a large cloth napkin. He smiles in full appreciation.

"Beer?" she asks after glancing at his hat and holds out a summer ale.

Centuries seem to fall away as Odysseus rests in that unkempt yard chewing warm pork and swigging golden beer. *Not much like a ghost anymore*, he muses as he finishes his third bottle. *This visibility is working out after all.*

The woman smiles. They have not exchanged names, he notes.

"Come inside and meet my kitties," she says. "There's plenty of room for us all."

※◆♒︎ℭ♏ℭ

There is trouble leaving a message, of course. Damned foreign travel! And she really wants to ask her Beloved if he remembers that little broken temple on the Skyros mountainside....

Alpha, beta.... The Novelist winces. Shaking her head she goes upstairs again to look at a guidebook and some photos they took. She still keeps albums, doesn't like computer files for pictures.

What was it about that man at GreenStar?

She pulls out a binder full of plastic pages and begins to feel nostalgic. Yes, the Aegean really did look fully bottle-green some days. And the blue of marbles other days, with the white foam like the hooves of horses....

Now she's reaching for Edith Hamilton and other books about mythology. Too much coffee? Too much tea? She's beginning to feel frantic. But *something* is pushing at the back of her head, an impulse, an emerging idea like the hard edge of a dream. *O, P, O, P, QQQ....*

Nope: no good to stay in the house. Absolutely no good. Maybe it's the barometric changes. Maybe it's because her birthday is less than three weeks away. Birth–that's it: she hasn't felt this kind of restlessness since her long-ago pregnancies. She was hungry then, too. Now all she wants is a big helping of Greek food...but she doesn't want to cook. Not yet.

Downstairs again. Raincoat over her arm, in case. Owl now in deep *skirt* pocket. Door closed. Key in car.

Just a few miles through Cayuga Heights, then bypassing Collegetown, then the bumpy bricks of Stewart Avenue, then down Buffalo Street and a left on Schuyler Place. As she turns right onto Seneca she is treated to a most unusual smell–wafts of roast rosemary pork–where a woman with tousled hair has begun to dismantle a barbecue in her front yard. The Novelist feels such a growl in her belly she is sure she has awakened the little owl.

Past The Commons, left onto Cayuga Street, and–miracle!–a parking space not far from the library. Now to deal with one of the new complicated pay-to-park machines the city decided to install in place of the convenient individual meters. What is her damned license plate number again?

Needing a break, Penelope wafts her way to the top of the stairs. She glimpses something in the hallway mirror as she passes but doesn't pay it much mind. She's intent on what she hopes is still available in the kitchen: a bag of pistachios tucked by a tenant into a cupboard over the stove. She's been dipping into them for several days, counting on the young man's fondness for marijuana to distort his recollection of quantity. Yes: there they are, just the salty green she needs at this moment.

Back upstairs, she feels despondent again, though. It seems to her that her poetry, instead of coming together, is beginning to unravel. Is she getting too personal? Drifting from history? Maybe she should go back again to the early years: her aunt, her cousins. But has she veered too wildly in surmise?

Leda's Young

I'll tell you about swans:
here in these fat golden eggs
they are everything to us.
We dream their thunder, wings

pulling the wind to their command,
our black father largest of all,
his scream a hurricane. Oh yes
we will become him. We will leave

our mother with her small frail
smiles, eyes searching the sky.

Hear this catalogue: crimson
dragonflies, weeds sceptred with jewels,

water a world that mirrors world
and takes it greenly deepward. Swans
do not have the grace to walk on land
and do not need it. Give us air

and lake, each blue edge and line
a surface we will break with ease
of feathered thrust. Within
this curve of shell already we can

feel our beaks begin, each sharp tooth
the means of shattering our way
to waiting power over all.
Listen. You will hear it, too:

the crack and smash of shining walls
falling fast around our chosen heads.

Always she must wonder what the exact and true blood
connections *are* among these history-shapers. Zeus the
father of Helen and Polydeuces? Tyndareus the father of
Castor and Clytemnestra? Or was it a mystical mix of two
couplings inside Aunt Leda's womb as she gestated on
Sparta, half-dreaming, half-fearing? She was married, yes,
and bore Timandra, Phoebe, and Philonoe to her husband.
But unlike so many other Hellenic women–Penelope's
mother, Periboea, for one–*wife* was not her limited destiny.
She must have had a wider life, damn it!

Leda, After

Before the swan, I knew everything
a girl should know about the world:
family, food, clothing spun with threads

from softest white and turned to rainbow
in dark pots of boiling dye. I
wasn't yet prepared for parenthood,

believed I had a few more years
of blood each month, freedom to run,
stories rising from heart's core

to teach me towards tomorrow. Sorrow
was another's song–mother's, sister's–
not the golden way of being

that shaped my voice, my hair. Dare I
boast now and say I was the blessed,
the lovely lily among leaves

that stained the watered world around me?
He–the one of darkest cloud
and hottest light–took wings for me

and trembled his swift menace lust
between my thighs, into my flight.
Night named the feathers He-Who-Seeks-

to-Lose, and I have kept them all

these years, under my tongue, wound
in a crown, scattered in my morning

hours when mothering shrieks out
my name and I recall the pure
long stretch of possibility

before sky tore, before blood rose,
before womb's swords of gold made sure
his thunder thrust me into fame.

Her fingers feel too tight, cramped, tired of her pen. Restlessly she gets up and decides to climb through the window and sit at the top of the black metal fire escape on the small platform that holds her pots of basil. She whispers the fragment of verse she has memorized, her reminder of the core of what she is writing:

And Leda was the mother
of two sisters: Helen,
prize for Paris when he declared
Aphrodite the most beautiful
and gave her the gilt apple;
and Clytemnestra, who slew
her husband Agamemnon,
greeting him with a victory carpet
dyed the royal hue.
And the Trojan War and all its tragedies
brought great unhappiness to Zeus...

She'd found these lines on a scrap of paper between the pages of a book in Autumn Leaves—a children's picture book about Hellenic heroes–stuffed next to a rough drawing of swans, with the word "Aal" scribbled in blue ink below the faded typed words. The name of a fellow poet? Odd, if so. A misspelled word of commentary? A scrawled prayer? No matter. She's kept the scrap of paper as a talisman, the catalyst for her summer's work.

As she stands up to go back through the window, she realizes her belly is growling. Lunch! She happily anticipates the plate of familiar food she will enjoy just half a block away, with some tasty salad on the side. Tomatoes, cucumbers, olives, feta–and the crunchy lettuce so decidedly *not* the cuisine of her country. Yes, the fact that The Souvlaki House is just a few steps north across Eddy Street was definitely a factor in her choice for a writing room. Odysseus likes eating there, too–and drinking the redolent red wine pressed from the Finger Lakes' vineyards.

She descends the stairs to the front door that leads to a wrap-around porch. To one side is a battered-looking storage area. She steps out onto a patch of mottled grass; plenty of rain has fallen this month—so different than the weather she was used to when she was alive and also from the unchanging skyless gloom of the Underworld—but still the small lawn is patchy and sparse.

As she crosses Eddy Street she looks up again at the sign she finds so reassuring:

Fine Italian & Greek Cuisine
Seafood & Steaks Since 1970
Gourmet Pizza * Subs * Salads * Pasta

Inside, only two tables are occupied. Slow August,

before the thousands of Cornellians she has heard about return–and besides, it's late for lunch. She's been working steadily for hours! Almost greedily, she goes as usual to help herself to bread and salad and moussaka or pastitsio from the kitchen, where it's easy to steal. But this time–

"May I help you?" an annoyed voice demands, clearly not wanting to "help" at all.

Penelope whirls to see one of the owners glaring at her. How is this possible? *Ghosts are invisible* she tries to tell herself again.

"Please take a seat in the dining area," the voice continues coldly. "We'll be glad to take your order *there.*"

Completely nonplussed–*he can see me!*–Penelope almost stumbles as she moves away from the kitchen. She can't even find the words to apologize. Would he even be able to hear them? *What is happening?*

As fast as she can she exits The Souvlaki House and, feeling naked and helpless, quickly re-crosses Eddy Street. She's thinking very fast. She has to get back into the rental house. She knows she can hide in her room—if none of the other tenants see her. *This cannot be! This should not be!* keeps ringing in her head. Fortunately, she knows, only a few of the other seven bedrooms became summer rentals, and much of the time during the day their inhabitants have been absent.

In a vigorous trot she makes it to the house and enters. Up the stairs and safely behind her door once more, she dares to go to the cluttered dresser and look into the spotted mirror attached to it. There she sees with horror a face with dark eyes, a head with silvered black hair, part of the owl printed on her dress. Is she going mad? Is it a sign that she and Odysseus are being called back early to the Underworld? *How can this be?!*

A chortle behind her makes her turn.

"Yup, quite a shock, eh, m'lady?" A very handsome youth in tight-fitting jeans and an *Ithaca Is Gorges* t-shirt is smiling widely at her.

"Wha–?" Penelope begins in dismay, then looks more closely. Her heartbeat settles a bit. "Hermes!" she almost spits out, in both anger and relief.

"Your hubby had a similar reaction," he responds with a delighted smirk. "No need for alarm, really. It's just for today. Athena's away celebrating Mary's Ascension Anniversary."

Still bewildered, but able to breathe more normally again, Penelope sighs. "And you're having fun with us about it, aren't you? Of all the…. Well, you can bet *I* certainly won't be going out of here again until I'm invisible again—but what about Odysseus?" She begins to realize just what this sudden change must mean for him, out and about in his usual way.

"Not to worry, dear poet. You just go back to your work. He's having himself a fine old time. And he'll make his way up here to you–eventually. Here: I snagged a gyro for your lunch to help you calm down."

And with a wink and another bright smile, before she can ask any more questions, Hermes is gone, a whiff of sexy aftershave lingering where he had stood posing in his golden Converse.

⁂

Among the many shapes and patterns of fur, Odysseus wakes from what he knows was not a dream. His groin aches, and he is certain there are fingernail scratches on his back. He finds his shirt, his hat, his pants–the well-wrapped vegetarian eggrolls still intact–and struggles into his deteriorating sandals. It feels like a year has passed. The taste of rosemary still lingers on his tongue. *Pigs*, he muses. *Men bewitched into pigs...so long ago.*

He leaves behind the cat-hair-covered futon stained with little moons of redolent piss and looks for its owner, to no avail. All he finds is a note tacked to the inside of the door: "Journey well."

Oddly, as he steps outside, a north wind is blowing, though the air is still heavy-hot. The grill has disappeared.

He decides he must find a place with shade, to breathe easy and to think. Across Schuyler Place he sees trees that remind him of an old olive grove, and he decides to risk trespassing. Hiding himself as best he can, he sits on the ground to ponder what is happening.

It *must* be his visibility. It *must* be because Athena is not here to protect him. Somehow the broken sandal epitomizes it. "Journey well"? What had that young woman expected of him? What did she want?

A child echoes in his mind, half-memory, her voice whispering those words into his ear as the cats mewled around them.

She had not known he is a ghost.

He cannot make children anymore.

On a branch high above his head, a crow starts cawing. The bird does not see him and he does not see the bird. When it flies off he gets up, crosses Seneca Street, and begins to move further up the hill. Wild grapevine chokes a bush in front of a house hung with a sign proclaiming "Apartment for Rent."

HOMER

After *three* reheated slices with spinach and feta at the gourmet pizza place on Cayuga and Green, the Novelist spends a good couple of hours in the quiet sanctuary of shelves and tables and chairs of the county library. She thinks fondly of the smaller pink one on Fleming Street in Key West, then focuses on figuring out why she's–yes, at this point–almost *haunted* by thoughts and memories of Greece. Where *had* that almost fierce-looking short man in GreenStar come from? His clothing looked Ithacan, but his physique, his way of walking...and even for the summer he was much too tan....

She finds herself writing out the alphabet again, down a page, and playing with planning out an acrostic poem. What's one called using the alphabet? Oh, yes: an abecedarian. She hasn't written poetry in decades, she thinks again. Of course, classically, long ago, *all* literature was called poetry, before distinctions embraced by critics (and librarians) made people trouble with labels. Didn't Homer really shape a novel, in verse? She wiggles her pen next to where she has set the owl out on the table.

> *All the birds of Athena rise*
> *by her temple on the mountainside*
> *carved in marble and looking far*
> *down to the sea where Thetis came*

Annoyed, impatient, she crosses out every word, very vigorously. *Stuff and nonsense,* she scolds herself. *You're a fiction writer. And you've got the awards to prove it.*

The little owl stirs and readjusts its wings as though it knows more than she ever could. As though, well, it is wise. It makes not a peep as she slips it back into her skirt pocket.

What is Penelope to do? Worry about her husband? She left that practice behind long ago after living it for too many years. No, she doesn't *feel* any different, so she decides to go back to what she is supposed to be doing, just like the old days at her loom–again waiting for Odysseus, if Hermes was telling her the truth.

Where did she leave off before trying to go to lunch? She nibbles at the gyro for inspiration, then returns to her folders, determined not to look into a mirror again but instead to keep shaping her poems.

Ah, yes: that goddess of love, selfish like almost all of them (Hestia the exception), mortals her playthings, toys to delight her and then be dropped, no remorse, no guilt, little memory. What *if* that jealousy with Hera and Athena had not arisen? As a shade, Penelope no longer has to fear reprisal; she writes what she will write.

Aphrodite

Long beauty, perfect beauty: only I
deserved the golden apple his hand cupped
in curving palm. To rock-slung hills, to high
pale walls and windowed halls where families supped
and women wove rich stories on tall looms
I carried him in dream, and there he found
the one I promised him. And if the rooms

around her were a king's, her choices bound
by marriage vow? No matter. Mortal time
commences, carries, ends like a thin poem
contained with meter, ruled by foolish rhyme,
unlike my own free dance of ocean's foam.
I wanted that bright prize, my power praised,
though men's blood tore their breath as towers
    blazed.

Much more difficult, she's found, has been to find a voice for her cousin. Gorgeous Helen, self-absorbed, helplessly vain–yet always Penelope has sensed her flaws came from a suppressed knowledge that she would be punished for her beauty, seen only *as* Beauty, used for a grand dangerous fate that would damage the world for many. Or is this speculation all hindsight? Penelope sighs. What she must do is focus on the goddess-swept passion that consumed her cousin, so different from the sensible tender commitment she herself made to Odysseus.

Helen

They say it was my face. No:
let me tell you about marriage.
Silences and swords, a stone house,
my women whispering around me
dull as bees. For years before he touched
our doorsill, I dreamt his voice;

the silver gifts he brought were tiny
mirrors of the girl I'd held inside
too long. Soon I turned willing hands

to weave for him, each thread a piece
of secret song. The peacock blue, the purple
heart of pansies, red a cry of sun

setting over unclimbed hills. *I asked
to go with him.* I knew he watched
me walk across cool tile, my feet
in sandals I yearned to kick away
so I could run to him unbound
by safe convention. Strange strong guest,

reluctant to offend the man he knew
I didn't love, whose hospitality
was heartless, rote, a hand that drops
coins in a beggar's cup without a glance.
One morning when the sun rose white
and helplessly again I moved to stand

beside him where the swans swim slow,
he took my hand in his and nodded *yes.*
All time burst to blossom and I
knew what it was to be the rose.
Swift ships, sting of salty air, my hair
wrapped around his fingers in the dark:

we could have lived forever in that place
of travel, seabirds wailing overhead,
the men around us eyeing me like some
pure stolen chance—how could they know?
—and my hopes free as any muscled gleaming fish
leaping higher than those blue and bitter waves.

Penelope pauses. She knows of what many do not know and what, therefore, so few have considered, let alone written about: the child Helen so suddenly left behind. How does a young woman deal with this kind of abandonment? Is she expected to remain silent, go on with her days as though nothing has changed?

Hermione

What does a daughter matter when a man
has claimed her mother? Puff of smoke. A hand
erasing her existence as waves can
eradicate scrawled letters in smooth sand.
She sailed to Troy without a last goodbye
and in my simpler beauty I was left
to bear the burning weight of her life's lie
beside my father, bitter and bereft.
I dreamed of her? Oh, yes, and Paris, too,
bejeweled and walking hand in hand through halls
where windows let pour sunlight from skies blue
above high strong protected golden walls.
She left me nothing but a broken loom
I stared at, hating, in my empty room.

And what *was* Helen's life behind the walls of Troy? Penelope has tried to imagine, tried to enter into her days and nights. Did her cousin erase memory, only to have it arise from her unconscious?

Helen Dreams About Her Mother

White, white hands—soft
as swan's-down, no, as clouds
the wild swans fly down from

to float upon clear water
where a heart-shaped boat awaits
her careful step. A man

with a basket full of sticks—
silver gray, shining, the shafts
of arrows, perhaps, thunder

turned to bone and glass?—
approaches her and whispers of
a pair of wings that soars above

all islands past the sun
to night. She laughs, tells him
to go away, begins

to sing a song of winter
sunlight thin on hills.
Helen stirs in her sleep

and moans, a star still stuck
in her throat from love,
pulls Paris ever tighter

on the pillow they share.
Tomorrow she'll wake and not
remember the waves and the woman

with her face, the girl
who ran ahead crying aloud
how much the feathers hurt.

And that Trojan, Hecuba's and Priam's son, hated by Hera and Athena because of his bribed judgment. Lover? Thief? Acquirer of Sparta's gift with looms? Penelope is aware that he, too, has been interpreted a thousand times. Can she offer with any accuracy the doomed young man so capriciously favored by Aphrodite? *Did* her cousin choose him, or was she bewitched?

Paris

Again her jeweled hair soft
and bright, her lover's promise:
True is all my words can know.
I remember her in sandals
gleaming on blue stone, her feet
a sure perfection walking
towards my waiting arms. *Love,*
how long I've waited for you
in this castle of closed doors.
We moved through dawn like light
through watered silk, her hands
strong and easy as she spoke.
See, here is where the swans
make nests, their wings a silent
home for small bright eyes.
She wanted me, I tell you;

all her days were made of dreams
of what could be. And I?
Mad adorer, midnight in my eyes.
Our first kiss held all my life
in question, and the answer
tumbled hard and fast toward death.
How a tongue can be a sword
swift and sharp to the heart:
Take me with you, my beloved.
We'll disappear like rain.

Surely too romantic, Penelope fears. Too forgiving. After all, Paris was the human agent of her husband's being forced to leave Ithaki, to roust out Achilles on Skiros, to gather warriors and ships and disappear into plunder and siege and bloodshed and fire, and then the god-cursed journey "home" that now famously bears his name.... She stops herself, suddenly, for this mental track always allows her bitterness to escape. Oh, she has worked so hard to imprison it, to keep it away from where she needs to be to write!

So often she has speculated how the course of history could have changed if Achilles' immortal mother *had* been successful in hiding him as a woman, if Odysseus had not been so very astute in offering swords along with jewels when he came to the court of Lycomedes.

On Skiros: Gray Stone Beach

In afternoon the light is careful here
to silver softly, giving this old land
a quiet way of being, calm and clear,

rocks rough and pebbles smooth to human hand.
Waves push and pull, to careful listening ear
a lullaby of hush on glistening sand,
cool comfort strong enough to calm long fear
and ask the heart to venture what's unplanned.
To come here all alone is to touch dream
when dream needs art's embrace; to walk with one
well-loved is to discover secret gleam,
and sharing this small shore with more, the sun
sets stories free: a hidden place, away
from easy path, where Thetis whispers *stay.*

But it was not so. So much was not so. Penelope stands up from her desk, moves around the room, careful not to look into the mirror again. Another nibble of the gyro to bring a feeling of warmth and good fortune? She doesn't dare venture for more pistachios. How to break out of this downward spiral of her own years of suffering? Think of other mortals *not* blessed by the gods, but punished instead?

Hubris.

Arachne, Weaving

When she sat down on her simple stool
what possessed her to stiffen her spine
and portray all the gods and goddesses
copulating where they shouldn't have
coupled with lovers they shouldn't have
loved? Foolish human, she embraced hubris
and flicked her hair back at Athena,
sure of her fine strong hands.
Deft Arachne, gifted Arachne: what could
She-Who-Rules-All-Looms do
but punish the vain girl? Shrink her down,
lengthen her limbs, fill her small belly
with poison. And finally, the perfect touch:
thin her vision so she can't see
the glittering webs that delight the world
mornings when she's worked all night
atoning for her bold wrong-fingered pride.

Nope. Not good enough. Too direct, explanatory. Penelope folds the page in half and writes REVISE–OR DESTROY in big block letters. Shrugging, she reaches for another page.

Cassandra

To know a snake, its very namelessness,
and warm it with your warmth: that's what
Apollo taught me. Me with my simple

parted hair and braids, girl-child with two
pitchers in my hands, balancing time of dream
and time of waking. He made me his

with his voice of light and face of music
and gave me the most dangerous power
a sky-god can bestow: *to see.* I should

have known the wings I felt at first
would drip with wax and falter, sure
as the lust he blazed toward me

met only stone beneath my silk.
I might have loved him if I could,
but what flesh can take such burn?

Truth a dead bell on my tongue
I fled the temple, his snarling curse
a hot hiss in my ears.

Apollo: yes, definitely a god to watch out for. Penelope
had always felt great sadness for Cassandra, whose fate
from the Trojan War was so drastically different than her
own. Agamemnon, Mycenae, Clytemnestra–yes, the two
women have talked of it often over the centuries, though
Cassandra always falls silent when it comes to recalling her
exact end at the hands of another betrayed woman.

Betrayal...sometimes conscious, sometimes not, muses
Penelope. She has written in the voice of another who died
young and then died a second time:

Eurydice

You turned: I tasted salt.
Gagging on it, choking, harsher
than any waves of the Aegean

we might have swum in, naked.
Your lyre, silent through all
our journey, fell to the ground

beside you. Death–again!
Did Hades and Persephone
plan it all along, smiling,

him full of bitter cunning,
her jealous, resentful, knowing
we could share full years

of love? Why couldn't they forgive
the bright snake's bite, my corpse
in my husband's arms? Allow

the light-torn stifled climb–me
in your shadow, shrouded, veiled,
an echo of your tongue's demise–

and let me know blood's flow again,
your perfect touch upon my brow,
your fingers, blessed fingers.

Just before Stewart Avenue a bed of tall ornamental grasses still harbors a few raindrops. Sound comes from the back of the house-sound very different than the radios blaring rap and heavy metal from the few passing cars. Song, Odysseus realizes, and he can't help drawing closer. And closer. Until he's leaning against the side of the house peering into the backyard...

...where two middle-aged women with guitars are rehearsing Linda Ronstadt songs. Clearly they are used to singing together. They look like sisters, in fact. Their voices are honey and gold and fresh mint. Odysseus just has to step up closer as they beautifully croon about doing everything they know to try to make a man theirs so they can love him for a long, long time without him breaking their hearts in two....

Suddenly Odysseus is aware of a loud silence. The music has ceased.

"Can we help you?" one of the women says, her voice tinged with ice. Her lush auburn hair spills down her back.

The other, seemingly a bit younger, with compelling large blue eyes, adds stridently, "This is private property, sir."

Still entranced—oh, he can't help but think of sirens—Odysseus finds himself smiling numbly. Then he's struck with inspiration. He lays on a heavy accent.

"Ladies, my apologies for intruding, but your music called to me. I am a visitor to Ithaca. I have come all the way from the other Ithaca—the island of Ithaki, in Greece."

The two singers gaze at each other, evaluating his request.

"Well," one says, shrugging, "that's unusual. I guess it's okay if you stay a bit."

"Yeah," says the other. "We're using our friend's backyard to rehearse for one of our shows. I suppose an audience can't hurt."

And so Odysseus dreamily stays, and listens, and once again is very glad he does not have wax in his ears.

☰ ◆ ≋ ☼ ♏ ☼

With images of gods and heroes and islands and seas pounding through her mind, the Novelist gets up to leave. On her way towards the exit she passes a community bulletin board, and a hand-lettered sign catches her eye:

EVERYTHING MUST GO YARD SALE
AUGUST 15 ONLY
712 E. SENECA (CORNER OF QUARRY)

Perfect! She has always liked a good bargain and enjoys rummage sales. Sometimes she gets a good story idea from what other people have abandoned. By now–she glances at the clock above the circulation desk and sees it is almost two o'clock–maybe things are half-price. *Unusual to have a sale on a Wednesday,* she thinks. *The people must be desperate to clear out stuff, maybe for a move. And students are beginning to come back into town now and need things for their apartments.*

Happy for the diversion, she walks through the opened glass doors, waits for the light, walks diagonally (illegally) across the intersection, and gets into her car. She almost feels like humming. The sky looks as though it might clear.

East on Green Street, then right onto Martin Luther King, Jr./State, where she passes the expensive Argos Inn,

70

designed to delight tourists and parents used to big-city prices for lodging. *Might as well head up to Eddy Street*, she figures, *and park close to Fontana's for after the yard sale.* She hopes they'll have the shoes she wants, and in her size.

The little owl seems more and more restless, but she reaches into her pocket and strokes its head to calm it.

Again lucky with parking–a miracle, really–she walks south on Eddy, noting the interesting scale-like pattern of shingles on the old house at the top of Seneca and the vibrant pots of basil high up on its fire escape. *The Greeks do that*, she suddenly remembers. *Basil at their doors for hospitality.* The little owl shifts its weight again.

Number 712 is a short walk down the hill, a bright yellow house with a large neatly-trimmed grass lawn. Nine wooden steps lead up to a small front porch. Why does the word *Ogygia* suddenly pop into her head?

She lets the thought go, though, because to her great satisfaction she sees six long tables standing on what used to be a side driveway, she guesses. The rush on the sale must have been hours ago, yet the tables are fully laden with what looks like centuries of goods. The Novelist's acquisitive instinct kicks in: what treasures might she find?

Thinking of the unfortunate bride bitten by a snake, Penelope can't help shivering, even in this full warmth of August. What if she and Odysseus had been separated when they left the Underworld together, somehow confused on purpose by Hades? Then another thought strikes her: what if Hades goes back on his word and decides to *punish* them for Odysseus's riddle, forcing one of them to remain in the world – *visible!* – while dragging the other back into his realm? It's very conceivable....

Go elsewhere, she thinks. *Another fictional character, who surely could have existed in the drama of her cousin's life as Menelaus's sequestered wife. A sad voice, but a safe voice.*

Helen's Handmaiden

She told me she adored him.
Who could doubt it, looking
at her eyes? Blue

sky after a storm,
fire in darkest night.
Hours we spent talking

at our looms, our voices
low and seeming casual.
The dreams her fingers worked

into her threads! She spoke
of wanting him so much
her breath came heavy, air

around her sharp and hard
enough to make her fall.
And I, unable to

unfold my own desire
—oh, her golden hair!—

I sat, and smoothed my gown,

and listened to it all.

After rereading this poem, Penelope muses: *Even without her beauty, I may well have been a secret desire for some of my weaving women....* Then she shrugs. More likely this fantasy has arisen as protection against the almost masochistic poems she's sometimes forced herself to write. Hmm...*will* she ever be able to write about Circe? Who bore Odysseus's son and killer, Telegorus, and thus widowed *her*, his wedded wife? Penelope has never again swum in the sea since her husband died from the spear made from the stingray spine. Yes, afterwards the melodramatic Fates coupled her with Telegorus and Circe with Telemachus—such strange, complicated, twisting memories, so long ago—but she always knew that just as she had waited for him, Odysseus had looked forward to their rightful reunion when death finally claimed *her*. Even so, every time she attempts a poem about Circe, it winds in upon itself and disappears....

✻ ◆ ≋ ♋ ♍ ♋

Odysseus, as though in a dream, keeps listening to the two sisters play, their voices like streams of light across smooth waves. When their rehearsal comes to an end, he rises and thanks them. Still entranced by the memory of their music, he is caught unawares when he returns to the sidewalk and finds himself smack in the middle of a probably-marital altercation next door.

"You jerk!" a wild-haired woman is screaming as she

stands in fury on a high bank next to the street. "I *told* you not to water the grass so much! That rain last night turned it into mud. It's sucked down all the roots! Not to mention all the garbage those students threw on it."

"Stop your bitching!" a dirt-smeared man retorts from below. "*I* told *you* not to use that goddamn power mower. It's ancient! And now it's torn up the lawn!"

"Oh, so it's *my* fault again, is it?" the woman shrieks. "Damn you!"

"Yeah, you and your fucking bargains! A piece of crap, that machine always has been. It's like a bloody monster! Blades like goddamn arms!" The man is almost spitting his words.

As if planned, again the mower roars as the woman starts it up, almost viciously shredding more grass, and the hose sprays water as the man whirls it in all directions, leaving pools in bare patches. Instinctively, to avoid the turmoil, Odysseus grabs at a tree trunk and swings up onto a branch as the couple stare at him in confusion.

He barely makes it, succeeding only by forcefully pushing his feet against the rough bark. And that is the cursed *end* of his sandals.

☙❦☙

Two other potential customers–strangers to each other, apparently–are leisurely picking up and putting down glass and wooden and ceramic and metal objects. Oddly, the Novelist discovers that any object she looks at directly seems to shimmer faintly into a kind of vagueness, like letters stared at by someone needing glasses. Only when she reaches out and actually touches an item–a lone beater for an electric mixer–does it take firm shape. Doesn't she need to replace a bent one at home, for baking later? The price is right–twenty-five cents–so she keeps hold of it in her hand as she turns towards another haphazard display.

What's this? Half a table offers what looks to be shoes, in pretty good shape. Some are even still in boxes. Could she be so lucky? The little owl stirs in her pocket as if feeling the exhilaration of the chase; the Novelist knows that motion and takes it as a sign of good fortune.

But no: not a twinkle of resemblance to the kind she wants. None even in her size, except for a pair of black patent leather boots studded with what look like glitter-painted thumbtacks–definitely not her taste.

Sighing, she twirls the metal beater between thumb and forefinger and goes to the table spread with books, always an inevitable perusing point for her at any rummage sale. None of the books shimmer the way other untouched objects are still doing. All of the titles in the hardcovers and paperbacks are clear. She always likes to play the game of "Have I read this one already? Do I have it in my library? Do I want to?" and, of course, "Did I write it?" Maria Tatar's *Annotated Classic Fairy Tales*. Well, she's quoted in that one. *Dragon Stories* by E. Nesbit. She's written essays about that one. A chapbook by an obscure local poet called *Dark Matters*, with a disturbing painting on the cover reminiscent of Little Red Riding Hood–that one's actually dedicated to her, she vaguely recalls. Interesting mix from whoever is selling these books. Most are by women. Could the ones by men have already sold? The Novelist smiles wryly. Then with mixed emotions her hand does close over one of her own, an early one about adultery in academia. Was it read? Why is it being discarded and sold for fifty cents? She opens the cover: yes, there's her autograph, but with no inscription.

Propping that book up face-front against others so it stands out well, she moves around the table. A paperback catches her eye–small, less than an inch thick, with a stylized bright painting of a man tied with rope to a mast while other men row the boat past an island where long-haired women draped in blue seem to be singing towards them....

The little owl suddenly attempts to escape her pocket, so forcefully that the Novelist drops the book onto the grass-tufted concrete. As she moves to resettle the bird, she glances around, hoping no one is watching her. Now she notices with some unease the unusually muscled woman who must be in charge of the sale.

"Can I help you?" asks the woman as if she's seen nothing strange.

The Novelist stares a few seconds, clutching her coat, then replies in a rush, "I'll take this mixer blade. I've got a quarter somewhere...."

The woman just smiles. "Oh, don't bother paying. Just take it. I'm almost done with the sale for today."

Just go away quickly now is how the Novelist hears these words. She stuffs her new possession into the pocket that does not hold her owl and turns toward the street. Her vision seems still to be muddled by shimmer. Surely that short man heading towards the table of shoes can't be the same one she saw at GreenStar?

Penelope has never learned in detail from her husband

about the witch who kept him from her for seven years. But she has heard and read about this time in his life–oh, yes, much too often, in facts and speculation–from all the bards and tale-spinners and novelists fascinated by what he had to "endure" while he was away from her. Given that she herself was restored to her hard-earned place beside Odysseus, she'd actually taken satisfaction in eventually imagining the thoughts of the lonely creature who inhabited that cave of luxury.

Calypso

Seven years I held him in my arms.
The island of my heart, once crag and briar,
blossomed green and white and filled the air
with sweetest herbs. I knew he longed for home

but still he touched my hair and face and kissed
my eager mouth. I would have changed the world
to make him mine forever, but what magic
could hold sway over the dream he kept

of Ithaki? I thought to give him sons,
make him the lord of all I ruled alone—
no. Always he turned his eyes away
beyond me, after sex, after each dawn

I thought I'd found a new sea in his eyes.
A ship he whispered even as his lips
sought mine in body's hunger. Seven years
and now I sing the sorrow of his name.

As Odysseus holds onto the tree he wonders if he's become invisible again, because the couple stops staring at him and starts going at each other again.

"You're a complete *drag!*" the woman screeches and then slams her way into a car and roars off as the fuming man glares once at the tree and shouts "You putz!" before stomping into the house with a crash of the door behind him.

So, not *invisible,* Odysseus reminds himself, feeling foolish. Gingerly–his feet are bare now–he climbs down the tree. His sandals lie in tatters in the foaming mud.

The egg rolls have a new shape now, but Odysseus surmises they're still edible. As he crosses the Stewart Avenue intersection, he again wishes he had money, for he spots an All-Beef Hot Dogs food truck near the northeastern corner, where a mobile of seven glittering suns dangles on the porch of a blue-gray house next to hanging baskets of red and yellow flowers. Several young people are waiting eagerly in line at the truck. Despite the earlier feast of pork, the smell of the sizzling beef is going straight to his belly. He sighs and moves on.

The hill steepens here as it heads toward Collegetown. Odysseus tries to make a joke to himself about Mount Neriton. But it's not very funny. His feet are beginning to hurt where he rubbed them on the tree bark.

Just a few blocks more until the end of the street. He suddenly feels very tired. Maybe, he thinks, the visibility is putting a strain on him.

That's when he gets to the northeast corner of Quarry Street. Set back behind a large neat lawn of well-trimmed grass is a bright yellow house–too bright, really–with a semicircular concrete path leading up to it. Nine wooden steps rise to a small front porch. A tree stands on each side of it next to white Corinthian-style wooden pillars.

These details register vividly, but it is what Odysseus sees on the eastern side of the yard that makes him stop walking. On cracked pavement with tufts of grass sticking through it stand half a dozen long folding tables covered with kitchenware and lamps and books and atlases and globes and frames–and *shoes*.

Only a few other people are milling around the tables, intent on bargains. He moves directly to the footwear, hoping. Black boots, brown boots, gray boots, tango heels, ballet slippers, running shoes–and one pair of sandals. Pink pleather. Children's size four.

Odysseus groans–and the sound seems to call forth the seller as though she's been waiting for him.

A petite woman of uncertain age approaches him, a purse full of cash slung around her hips. Odysseus notices the taut strength of her arms. *She works out*, he thinks. *Maybe even a bodybuilder.*

"And what can I interest *you* in today?" she asks. "I've brought something of everything out of my 'cave.' Students are coming back. But you don't look like a student."

Her eyes are light green and a little crooked, but Odysseus gets their message all right as they travel up and down his body. She's glad he's not a student.

"I was hoping for sandals," he says, indicating his naked feet. "A little accident took them as I was coming up from the west end of town."

"Hmm...nothing suitable on the table, I'm afraid." Her smile is a little crooked, too. "But why don't you come inside and look? I have years and years of stuff in there, including some of my father's clothes. He was a strong man in the circus and they liked to dress him up as a god."

Odysseus does a double-take. Who *is* this woman? One of Hermes' jokes? But she just turns and leads him into the house. From the entryway he glimpses shining glass lampshades and fat tasseled couches in a large room. The air is tinged with what might be incense.

"Let's go upstairs," she says. "By the way, my name is Callie."

"I'm Gnomon," he is careful to tell her, then follows her to the second floor.

She takes him into a peaceful room that smells pleasantly of lavender. A wide massage table waits in its center.

"This is where I work," she says. "But I've stored stuff in this closet."

Using a step stool she reaches for a large cardboard box and easily lifts it down to the floor. Odysseus stands a bit awkwardly until she tells him, "Just sit on the edge of the table. Let's see what we have here." She rummages. "No...no...no...well, maybe...," she says almost to herself. "Here. Try these."

As soon as Odysseus sees the sandals he knows they are too big–Titan-sized, he might almost say–but Callie is insisting he try them on. But first, she says, she must wash his feet. Then rub his feet. Then rub his legs ("Quite the scar you have there, eh?" she says softly). Then he must take off his clothes and lie down full-length so she can massage him properly ("With a little music playing, of course"). Then she must turn the lights down low. Then she must take off *her* clothes and climb onto the table beside him. Then she must make love to him as though she could make him immortal even though his mortality is long past....

In a daze of ecstatic pleasure Odysseus becomes gradually aware that he and Callie are no longer alone in the room. Like static electricity he feels another presence, then dimly sees the figure of Hermes standing with his arms crossed, an amused frown on his face.

"Naughty, naughty," his great-grandfather whispers.

Odysseus blearily attempts a reply, but Hermes cuts him off. "I mean *her*, not *you*. Do you have any idea how long you've been here?"

Still groggy, Odysseus slowly moves off the table, where Callie is sound asleep, smiling as she lightly snores. With Hermes "tsking" softly, he gets dressed, and then in a quiet flash both are back at the yard sale tables, now abandoned. In his stupor Odysseus trips over a fish tank but catches himself on a white silk belly-dance veil hanging from a coatrack.

When he is upright and looks again, Hermes is gone–as is much of the afternoon. And another thunderstorm is starting. He's still dazed, but carefully–aware of his still-bare feet–moves down the yard's slope to the sidewalk. Penelope, he realizes, has no idea of what's been happening to him. Again.

Instead of heading back uphill to Fontana's, the Novelist, feeling a bit rattled, decides to find a place to sit and have another cup of tea to clear her head. Maybe it's the weather–she can sense another thunderstorm beginning to build–but this day has become decidedly *odd*. If her Beloved were home from India all would be quite different, she thinks. When he is with her, days are not *odd*.

Well, why not just continue downhill? It's been years since she has climbed up or down Seneca Street. And she's never been to that new place–the Alley Cat Café?–just up from Aurora.

A short walk and she's crossing Stewart Avenue. Now she can fully see why her car suffers whenever she drives on this street: red bricks, gray pavement patches, and *potholes* big enough to turn any travel over them into an outback-journey experience. Hadn't the mayor made promises about repairing them in his campaign speeches?

Taking her time, she enjoys noticing the hanging baskets of flowers–two yellow, one red–that brighten the blue-gray house at the intersection, and then a bed of tall ornamental grasses in the 600 block. Maybe she should write a book about myths associated with flowering plants, like the one she wrote years ago about constellations. And put it into alphabetical order? She shakes her head. *Odd* idea.

As she gets close to the 400 block there's the decided smell of barbecue still lingering in the air, but no grill is in sight. It's enough to get her belly rumbling again a bit. Those slices of pizza weren't so very big. Maybe the café will have scones. Or baklava?

The little owl stirs in her pocket again. *Why* so active today? The Novelist gently takes him out and he almost glares at her, then ruffles his feathers and climbs up onto her shoulder. Maybe he's just needed air. But it's *odd* that he's so awake.

She pauses at number 420 to admire the dark orange door on the white house with black trim. She had enjoyed very much writing her book about houses, maybe even more than the one about clothing–but maybe that was just because she had become more seasoned. The Virgo in her appreciates details–like the heart-shaped gray stone, maybe a foot by a foot-and-a-half in size–artfully surrounded by plants and mulch in front of number 418 and the tightly constructed stone wall free of masonry that defines the driveway of number 408. Right now she'd welcome sitting on the big porch of that lovely cream-colored house. Certainly different from her also-appealing winter home in Key West.

Close to where the hill of Seneca Street begins, she passes a purple door to a basement apartment labeled "Purplefish Properties, LLC." She has no idea what that business is but thinks that if she *were* a poet she might use the phrase for a title. *Maybe about a sea creature with a deadly-sharp tail,* she muses. Where did that thought come from? The little owl makes a chirping sound almost like a burp, right into her ear.

Red petunias, with a few white–and then she's at the Alley Cat Café. She's heard that it takes its name from the unusual offering of time with adoptable cats–five dollars per half-hour–especially appealing to college students lonely for their pets back home–so she sagely decides to remain outside at one of the white tables. Humans cannot see her little owl, but cats can, and very eagerly.

Soon after she gratefully takes a seat, a server emerges with a menu in hand. She's relieved; she'd worried she might have to go inside to order. This young man is extraordinarily good-looking–she wonders if he might be a theatre major at Ithaca College–and his smile truly dazzles beyond cliché.

"Good afternoon," he says gaily–but then looks at her and stops speaking.

Alarmed–suddenly fearing that somehow he's seen her owl–she stares back at him wordlessly.

"Excuse me," he almost stutters. "It's just–well–you're–this is an unbelievable coincidence–I'm just now reading your book." And from his apron pocket he pulls a paperback copy of one of her books, a novel set partly in Key West. "I've actually been thinking of scripting it for a chamber theatre production at the Hangar. I want to play the carpenter."

The Novelist has never seen such awe on any face before. Part of her is flattered, of course, but her suspicious part is now absolutely sure he *is* an actor. Flamboyant. Over-the-top.

"Well," she says rather primly. "I'm sure that's very nice of you. You've asked my agent and publisher for permission, of course."

The young man's smile dims slightly. "Oh–well–you see–it's just in the beginning steps–I *will*, of course–and yours, too...." His voice trails off uncertainly. "But will you please sign it for me?" He seems almost to blush.

The Novelist, on familiar territory now, accepts the book from him with an automatic "I'll be glad to" and takes hold of the pen he pulls from his pocket. "And your name is?"

His smile dazzles again. "Herme," he announces, "With an accent over the *e*."

Just as I thought she muses. *Affected.* She quickly writes the inscription and hands him back the book and his pen.

"And now I'd like a cup of black chai, please, if you have it, with milk," she says. "And what pastries might you have?"

His voice flows like liquid gold. "Double chocolate cake," he croons. "Or–our special, today only–fresh *bougatsa*."

The little owl lifts his wings as if in some kind of triumph.

⁘⁘⁘⁘⁘

Feeling weary, Penelope pulls herself away from her pages and finishes the last of the gyro. Now she's longing for a wedge of baklava–super-sweet with honey and walnuts—to delight her tongue. What time is it? The afternoon is almost gone, she realizes, though much light still remains. How has Odysseus been faring? Again she must ask, "Where is he?" as she is reminded of how abandoned and vulnerable she felt, surrounded by the suitors with no divine help, unlike her husband who was guided by a protector. That protector who champions males has always seen Penelope as secondary, of course, only an extension of her favored mortal.

When the Owl Comes

she shivers, sometimes, Penelope,
fearing the beak that might share word
of death at sea or on an island
of wolves or one-eyed giants.
Love as love is often defined
has kept her well and weaving,
Ithaki's fine grapes and goats
thriving by her hand. But when
round golden eyes appear

and mighty striped wings settle,
what is she to make of night
as the goddess who has claimed her husband
softly hoots her name?

Too fixated on old resentment, she realizes, Penelope tries to go in a different direction, reaching for dark humor, always a struggle for her. What about that dream she's had several times? Why shouldn't she turn it into a poem?

Throwing Rats

It's one of her warmest midnight dreams:
grabbing rodents by the thick of their necks
and hurling them hard into the suitors
to watch who will grimace and who will shriek
and who will run away at last
from their torture of her free will.

Bat-black eyes, tremulous whiskers,
big bellies full of grain and grapes:
how they inspire ripe lust for revenge,
anger full as round casks of dark wine.
If only Odysseus could or would return.
If only their son were older, stronger.

Weak wishes: instead when her loom's undone
threads woven slowly from dawn to dusk
she sleeps alone in her marriage bed
where supple gray beasts climb the sturdy tree
he chose as post near her fine pillow

embroidered with ships she'll never see.

Odysseus is able to travel only one more block before heavy rain makes him run for shelter on the porch of a house that sports a handwritten sign: "$1,215 per month one-bedroom rental for graduate student." Yet another landlord seeking a tenant! As he stands there, clothes soaked enough to make him feel naked again, a young woman dashes toward the house from her car, keys in hand. He's about to apologize for being on her property, but quickly she says, "You poor man! You'd better come in. I'm sure my father will want to help."

Surprised and grateful, Odysseus enters the house with her and gladly accepts a thick towel. As he is drying himself off, the young woman returns with a glass of wine for him. Such true hospitality, and for a stranger! Surely these people embrace the Hellenic spirit. The young woman's father is polite and generous, and Odysseus finds himself talking a bit about what he has been experiencing. Clearly this household, like his own in the old days of Ithaki, has wealth. No hardship for the family to give him fresh clothes–albeit without sandals–and even a nice bit of cash when they learn he has none.

Father and daughter wish him the best as he ventures out once more. As he's leaving, Al—what his host said to call him–suggests he go to Fontana's on Eddy Street for new shoes.

"They're having their annual sidewalk sale. It's a good longtime Ithaca business," Al says. "Their slogan is 'Since before you were born'."

Odysseus smiles. *I doubt that*, he thinks, but thanks Al for the kind advice.

To her almost surprise, the young actor-director never appears again to bring the Novelist her pastry and tea. Instead a pleasant young woman–nice smile but nothing radiant about it–comes out with a tray decorated with images of slender cats.

"Stay as long as you like," she says. She glances at the sky. "And if that storm hits, just come on inside."

The Novelist thanks her, knowing she cannot go inside. She studies the sky appre-hensively. Thunderclouds are piling but they are still a distance away. And the air doesn't have that heavy stillness it gets just before rain starts.

With a sleepy hoot only she can hear, the little owl clambers down her raincoat and into the waiting pocket. The Novelist calmly sips her tea. And the *bougatza*–delicious. She realizes she hasn't had one since Skyros, from the little bakery where three streets meet in the village. Who is baking them here?

She pulls a notebook from her bag and jots down, "Consider writing a book called *The Language of Bakers*." She knows some of the facts about the history of wheat. More research would be enjoyable. And how about the tie-in to "Hansel and Gretel"?

When the server returns, the Novelist pays her bill but continues to sit at the table. Across the street is the long-established modern-furniture store, Contemporary Trends. She'd thought about giving a reading there when her book about houses came out, but–ha, ha, weak joke–there weren't enough places for people to sit and listen. Now, just east of it, another huge hotel is going up, a real giant. It's dwarfing the excellent independent family-oriented Community School of Music and Arts. *Progress....*

The café is comforting, but the Novelist realizes she should really get going. That sky *is* gray, and now she has hundreds of steps to make–uphill–in order to get to her car. Her main exercise has been to swim, but she knows the walk will be good for her. Thigh-tightening. And she doesn't have to rush.

The little owl is like a warm stone in her pocket as she begins her journey. She'd prefer to take her coat off, but she doesn't want to disturb the bird. He's finally sleeping soundly, she can tell.

Something about the pattern of her walking, the rhythm, pushes the alphabet into her mind again. Virginia Woolf's father and *Q*. She knows she's still stuck at *O* and *P*: what should she write next? A novel, a history–or something shorter? An essay? A novella–a novella about an *odd day*. But her mind skitters away just like the squirrel she startles as it descends a tree trunk.

Her ascent up Seneca is definitely more taxing than her descent. And she's not twenty or forty or sixty or even eighty anymore. She does take her coat off, folding it carefully over one arm without rousing the little owl. She can feel herself sweating as, yes, now the air is becoming heavier, denser. To the north she hears a low rumble. A monarch butterfly sails past her rapidly as though in search of cover.

Perhaps she should not have attempted this walk. She thinks longingly of her red car and of Fontana's Shoes, both secure and dry. She is moving so slowly now that she has plenty of time to notice the profusion of mushrooms in yards and on tree bark from recent frequent rainfall.

Nonsense: she's in excellent shape, and she has her coat with a hood. She focuses on the alphabet again.

The first fat, heavy drops catch her unawares. As she unfolds her coat to put it on, the sky rips apart with lightning and thunder, not quite overhead yet, but coming fast. She dare not stand near a tree. Checking for traffic she moves off the sidewalk and into the street. She passes where the yard sale was–tables now securely covered with (shimmering?) white plastic–and makes it to the next block. She'd only vaguely noticed the big Tudor-looking house before in her eagerness to reach the sale. Now she looks with great interest at its white stucco with brown trim and intricate windows. Shelter?

As quickly as she can she makes her way to the front door and knocks. And knocks again. No response. Well, at least she can stand here, with a little protection, as the rain pelts harder and harder from an almost-black sky. Amazingly, the little owl does not stir. She gently curves her hand around him to make sure he's still alive.

Already she's begun to think of how she will describe this adventure to her Beloved. Maybe they will *both* write about it.

In her heart of hearts Penelope does believe that Odysseus wanted to escape Circe's love spells, her seduction. After all, he *did* return to Ithaki and Telemachus and her. And he's told her (many times, actually) what it felt like to touch the shore of their island, to know that at last he had arrived. The demise of his dog *was* sad for him, though.

Homecoming

So dry, so waterless, he was almost salt
himself, dragging away from long sea
up the beach of rounded stones
where flowers so redolent of land
made him doubt the truth of waves.
Almost twenty years–who was he now?
Ithaki like a myth made real
as his rough nakedness touched it.
Who was the woman he'd left behind?
What son might dare to know him?
And that ragged beast, its tail awag:
thirsting, too, as Death lay ready
to carry loyalty into peace.

Without wanting to, almost wishing she had never written the next poem, Penelope has no choice but to turn to it as the inevitable companion to any account of her husband's return. Oh, the darkness of that day when Odysseus revealed himself, the aftermath still an obsidian blade in her heart! The girls and women who did *not* survive her husband's and son's vengeful wrath? Penelope's throat tightens. But it *is* part of the history....

Blood

I've heard about others' sons:

the grape, the poppy.
And what of Telemachus,
such a changed young man?
His eyes that used to seek
my face now stare beyond me:
over my shoulder, to the side
of my cheek, somewhere inside all
he needs, far past what I can give.

He has hanged them, my women:
dead eyes, dead tongues.
Why did he believe they had
betrayed us because of love?
They helped me keep the men
from seeing that my weaving
came to nothing, loosened
threads. They were my loyal allies,
young companions, almost friends.

Odysseus as father:
empty door, whispered hope.
I held on to all I could;
can a mother do more?
Telemachus so cold,
years of fury, loss.
Standing there now
with that sharp-eyed man,
both strangers, each alone.

Especially in the mist that's arisen after the storm,

Odysseus feels almost disguised in his new clothes: a blue cotton button-down shirt and gray sweatpants, no hat now. He certainly has quite the tale to tell Penelope (well, probably not *all* of it). Amazingly he's managed to salvage the egg rolls; they've become almost a talisman to him now.

He is so close now–not much more than a block to Penelope's writing room–but he stops to hold his hand out to an old dog eagerly trotting towards him and wagging its tail. He has never forgotten how Argos waited for his return. This dog is very different–never a hunter, Odysseus is sure–but with big dark eyes and a joyous tongue and ya-gotta-just-give-me-some-lovin' all over him.

The dog accompanies him as he continues. Up ahead he can see and hear at least two dozen young people milling about–students, surely, some wearing red hats bearing the letter *C* in white, most in expensive sandals. All look vigorously drunk. They are partying outside the two worn houses across from each other at the top of Seneca. Wait: one of those houses is where Penelope's room is. He becomes uneasy. If she doesn't yet know she's visible, might they see her? As he gets closer his worry increases: surely Penelope must be hearing the noise as one of the young men kicks repeatedly at the door of her house, swearing.

"Who's got the fucking key?" he calls out loudly. "There's more beer inside. I'm thirsty!"

As he turns to the others near him, though, his attention is suddenly pulled from the door. He glares at Odysseus, who is approaching the group now.

"Hey, old man, whaddya doin' with my dog?" he demands in a slurred voice. Startled laughter from the others follows. "That's *my dog*. He got out again. Ran away."

Odysseus stops walking. "The dog came to me," he says with dignity. "I thought he might be lost. He seems very needy."

"Nah, I bet you were tryin' to steal him," his confronter snarls, placing his fists on his hips. "Give him back."

"Oh, Antin," pipes up a young ponytailed woman hanging on another man's arm. "Who cares?" She burps, then giggles when her companion slaps her playfully on the buttocks. "He's old and he stinks and he's gonna die soon anyway."

"Just like this guy," her companion says as he crushes a beer can and tosses it into the street near Odysseus's bare feet. "Both losers."

By now the whole party is gathered near the pale yellow house, enjoying the drama. Most are gleefully smiling. One turns and vomits.

"Let him *have* the dog, Antin," the burping woman continues. "I've always hated the filthy thing. The landlord says we have to get rid of it anyway."

"But I don't *want* him to have the dog. I don't like his *face*," sneers the dog's owner. "Just look at him. That skin. He might be an Arab. Maybe a terrorist. Certainly doesn't belong *here*."

He steps awkwardly toward Odysseus–and dares to push him.

The dog whines, cowering.

The students have gone very still. Time seems to cease.

Anger is too small a word for what fills Odysseus. His chest goes tight; his breath burns. He wants to slay every one of these arrogant takers. He wants to see their blood flow. He wants to see the men in agony and the women hanging by their necks....

No, no—he is past this kind of action. He just has to make sure Penelope is all right. He works to control himself, not make eye contact with the people surrounding him. Some of them begin to pull away, probably assuming nothing more will happen, wanting to go back inside and drink some more. But then the one who vomited laughs loudly, picks up a small branch brought down by the storm, and raises it as if to strike both the dog and Odysseus–

"ZSAKISZEITE PALIOPAIDA!" Odysseus bellows with all the rage from all the pain he's ever endured. "FYGETE APO DO KAI SZO DIAOLO NA PATE! ZI KAZARA MOY NA 'XETE ESEIS KAI OPOIOS AGAPAZE!"

Bending down, he grabs a thin metal pipe lying on the ground, rears it back, and hurls it with the force of a bowstrung arrow. It flies straight and true directly across the street and smashes through a window, throwing glass in all directions.

Within sixty seconds, amidst screaming, all of the young people have fled back into the house on the other side of Seneca with a resounding slam of the door. The frightened dog, confused and whining again, huddles against Odysseus's legs.

"Good boy," he says soothingly as he begins to calm down. "We'll find a place for you. How do you get along with cats? As for you and me, we'll see each other again soon. Say, I'll bet you're hungry. How about a couple of squished egg rolls to help you calm down?"

✻

Time has become so distorted in this deluge that the Novelist truly cannot tell how long the storm has lasted.

Gradually the thunder moves on, the rain lessens, the sky begins to clear, yet a mist in the air remains. The side of her where her little owl is sleeping is relatively dry. Water soaked through on the other side. Well, once she gets to her car she can take off the coat, settle the bird on the passenger seat, and then go to Fontana's to replace her soaked shoes with brand-new ones.

As she leaves the doorway of number 808 and returns to the sidewalk, a ragged dog crosses her path. She steps aside just in time before he vigorously shakes himself, spattering muddy rain in contentment. Determined now to *get to her car* she leans into the final block of the hill–but then is halted by an altercation up ahead.

"Hey, old man, whaddya doin' with my dog?" she hears.

For one wild moment she thinks she has been mistaken for a man and is the one being confronted, but then she realizes that whoever is being addressed is surrounded by a group of young people–Cornell students, presumably, and obviously drunk. She can't quite see the man but does see a dog cowering nearby–surely the same one that shook itself as she passed it. Does he need help? What should and could she do? Apprehensive, she stops walking and monitors the encounter from a distance away. Is someone threatening the man, pushing him? Suddenly a laughing student picks up a branch and brandishes it–as a weapon?

Her question is answered by the man himself, who suddenly almost explodes with rage and yells at his attackers, "BACK OFF! GET THE HELL AWAY FROM US! A CURSE ON YOU AND ANYONE YOU LOVE!" And then what looks like a metal pipe goes sailing across the street and hits a window.

The Novelist stands in shock. Not because of the near-attack. Not because of the fury and loudness of the man's words. But because he uttered them in Greek–a language she does not speak–and she understood them.

And now that the students have run away, she can see the man–and recognize him. *Of course*, she thinks. *Who else could it be today?*

Ж◆ᴟ♋ℳ♋

Enough! Put the dark words aside! Penelope is all too aware that any day now–perhaps even tonight–Athena or Hermes or both of them will return and say, "Time's up!" and escort Odysseus and her back to the Underworld.

One more poem–perhaps a postscript?–to bring her manuscript to closure. A tribute to her aunt, words that might hold truth beyond the grave.

Leda as an Old Woman

No one remembers any more
how I flew through stars
to find my name, carried

the basket with seven stones
until each turned to pure crystal.
The swan was nothing, you

understand–a jab and thrust
quickly dismissed, black feathers
loose on the ground—no matter

he called himself Thunder Strikes,

air hissing in his beak.
What I mean is the way

gold flowered in me, all
my shadows dancing wild
as one, two, three, four

mouths and hearts took shape
to give me wings. *Free*:
how many women ever know

full bend and stretch of that
blue word? My children brought me
sky, a deathless journey past

their own destruction (even bitter
tears subside) and made me Queen
Forever of all colors, all light.

Penelope stands, paces around the room. Past is past, future is future: time is always present. History circles. What does that truth mean for her poetry? *Should* she bring it back to the Underworld and read it aloud to other ghosts? Throughout eternity she could keep writing them over and over again, add new ones for the dead.... But _no_! She craves a living audience, people whose choices they might affect. Suddenly she smiles.

In her neat handwriting, in her strong blue folder wrapped in black elastic, she will leave her poetry in the Argos Inn, propped up near the white moth. Someone will find it. Open it. Read it. Care?

As Odysseus feeds the dog, wondering exactly how he is going to get to his wife's writing room in his corporeal state, a familiar majestic figure suddenly takes shape before him.

"Hello, traveler," the goddess says, and with one wave of her staff she makes him invisible again. The dog, unfazed, continues to remain by his side.

"Penelope, too?" he asks.

"Yes. Already done," Athena replies with a smile. "Now I'm *really* tired." She yawns to prove it. "Oh, and by the way, the shoe store across the street is open until nine. They have nice sandals there." She disappears.

With a grin, Odysseus easily enters the house, climbs the stairs, knocks. Penelope opens the door and happily points at the empty mirror. "I heard a lot of noise," she says. "Banging. Your voice yelling. But I figured I couldn't do much about it." She smiles. "By the way, I finished my book."

"I brought you egg rolls, but they didn't make it in the rain. I fed them to the dog that's waiting outside."

"I bet you've got a bunch of stories from today. And, hey, I finished my book."

Odysseus raises an eyebrow. "Am I in it, my faithful bride?"

Penelope stares at him, straight-faced. "Is that a riddle, hero?"

Back at home that evening, with two pairs of exactly the kind of shoes she hoped to find, the Novelist relaxes with spanakopita from the Souvlaki House and a large salad with feta and olives. She pours her second glass of Aphrodite white from Northside Wine and Spirits.

Yes, yes, she thinks. *An* odd *day. Impossibly, a perfect day. O and P and, yes, she has found what she needs. It has begun. Ithaca will have a new novel. But it won't be all prose fiction. No, not after what she found herself writing, to her amazement, as soon as she returned home.*

Her little owl, fully awake again, regards her with compassion and trust. "Q-who! Q-who!" he tries to sing.

"Go for it, Glaukopis!" she replies, grinning. "And now listen to my poem."

The Dream of Odysseus

I listen to the wind from year to year.
Familiar faces haunt me through these days
of singing through the storms. I silence fear

as boats drift toward the invisible pier
and masts keep time above my weary haze.
I listen to the wind from year to year

though lean times stalk me from the past. I near
the shore after suffering the delays
of singing through the storms. I silence fear

and gather the frayed sails of my career
as the minotaur dreams in Mino's maze.
I listen to the wind from year to year.

Grace and fortune have kept my home sincere
and loving you has shown me all the ways
of singing through the storms. I silence fear

as the rudder cuts the water. I steer
clear of dark horizons, recite a phrase:
I listen to the wind from year to year.
I sing through storms. I silence fear.

ACKNOWLEDGMENTS

Adanna: "Regretting Pomegranates"

Ann Eliza Bleecker: An Anthology in Memoriam (Bristol Banner Books): "Leda as an Old Woman"

The Comstock Review: "Leda, After"

Cooweescoowee: "Aphrodite" and "Blood"

Deus Loci: "On Skiros: Gray Stone Beach"

Earth's Daughters: "Penelope"

Freshwater: "Zeus"

Hera: "Leda's Legacy"

The Hollins Critic: "Leda's Sister and the Geese"

Korone: "Leda Comes to Understand the Rain," "Helen's Handmaiden," and "Cassandra"

Nimrod International Journal: "Helen"

The Ocotillo Review: "Throwing Rats"

Orpheus and Company (University Press of New England): "Cassandra"

The Poets' Touchstone: "Paris"

Quiet Diamonds: "The Dream of Odysseus"

Skyros (FootHills Publishing): "Stones"

Talking River Review: "Calypso" & "When the Owl Comes"

Many thanks to Artists Embassy International, the California State Poetry Society, *Cyclamens and Swords* (Israel), *Korone*, The Poetry Society of America, and the Poetry Society of New Hampshire for awards that helped to forward the writing of this book. Thanks to the Argos Inn of Ithaca, New York for a wide-window-lit room (and, oh yes, the moth).

Special appreciation to Andres Hermida for providing the riddle (courtesy of Alejandro Jodorowsky and Salvador Dali) that freed Odysseus and Penelope from the Underworld, and to Ioanna Vargianiti for assistance with Greek (and for determining what Penelope's favorite garment would be), and to Eric Machan Howd for permission to include as the Novelist's his villanelle "The Dream of Odysseus." Thanks to Alexis Kale for her contributions as editor.

All elements in this novella are fictionalized except for the ghosts of Odysseus and Penelope, the poems by Penelope, and the author's name. This book's journey began on 27 June 2006, sojourned on several islands of time, then embarked on its completion after a blessing from Dina Glouberman on Skyros in the summer of 2018, arriving on shore in 2020.

About Atmosphere Press

Atmosphere Press is an independent, full-service publisher for excellent books in all genres and for all audiences. Learn more about what we do at atmospherepress.com.

We encourage you to check out some of Atmosphere's latest releases, which are available at Amazon.com and via order from your local bookstore:

Saints and Martyrs: A Novel, by Aaron Roe

When I Am Ashes, a novel by Amber Rose

Melancholy Vision: A Revolution Series Novel, by L.C. Hamilton

The Recoleta Stories, by Bryon Esmond Butler

Voodoo Hideaway, a novel by Vance Cariaga

Hart Street and Main, a novel by Tabitha Sprunger

The Weed Lady, a novel by Shea R. Embry

A Book of Life, a novel by David Ellis

It Was Called a Home, a novel by Brian Nisun

Grace, a novel by Nancy Allen

Shifted, a novel by KristaLyn A. Vetovich

Because the Sky is a Thousand Soft Hurts, stories by Elizabeth Kirschner

ABOUT THE AUTHOR

Z. K. Goat has been writing and publishing their poetry and prose for more than half a century. They have climbed to the temple of Athena on Skyros and to the palace of Odysseus and Penelope on Ithaki. They live by a long lake in central New York State.